Somersaults
— and —
Dreams

GOING ★FOR★ GOLD

CATE SHEARWATER

EGMONT

EGMONT

We bring stories to life

Somersaults and Dreams: Going for Gold
First published in Great Britain 2016
by Egmont UK Limited
The Yellow Building, 1 Nicholas Road, London W11 4AN

ISBN 978 1 4052 6902 5

www.egmont.co.uk

A CIP catalogue record for this title is available from the British Library

56727/7

Typeset in Sabon by Avon DataSet Ltd, Bidford on Avon, Warwickshire
Printed and bound in Great Britain by CPI Group

Stay safe online. Any website addresses listed in this book are correct
at the time of going to print. However, Egmont is not responsible for
content hosted by third parties.

Please be aware that online content can be subject to change and websites can
contain content that is unsuitable for children. We advise that all children are
supervised when using the internet.

Somersaults
— and —
Dreams

GOING
★ FOR ★
GOLD

For all the West Country League A squad girlies, past and present: Eva, Georgia, Gaia, Nancy, Camille, Esme, Niamh, Phoebe, Livvy, Isobel, Abby. And Elsie, of course!

And for Lynne Hutchison whose remarkable return from injury inspired this story and who continues to inspire young gymnasts across the country.

Thanks.

CHAPTER
One

Ellie Trengilly stood in the middle of the biggest gym she'd ever seen in her life. A vast white space with a sea of blue mats spreading out in all directions, white brick walls stretching up to viewing balconies and vaulted ceilings, and an arch leading to a pitted area. The National Sports Training Centre was all so shiny-new and high-tech that if Ellie's heart hadn't been bursting with excitement, she would almost have felt homesick for the familiar tatty surroundings of her old Academy. Almost.

Ellie still couldn't believe she'd been offered a place in the Junior GB gymnastics squad! Only twelve girls qualified for that honour each year. It meant they were invited to attend National squad camps like this one: a week of intensive training with top coaches at the National Sports Training Centre. It meant they were entitled to wear the coveted GB leotard, and it might – just might – mean a chance to compete for their country.

Of course, that was still a distant dream – for now, just being invited to National squad camp was enough for Ellie, as well as the fact that she was there with some of her best friends from the London Gymnastics Academy! Sweet, sensible Bella and Kashvi the tomboy were there, and even crazy little circus girl Katya had been offered a place – incredible, since she'd only started formal gymnastics training less than a year ago. And then there was Scarlett, Queen of the Beam – although Ellie didn't really consider her a friend!

Not all of her old Pre-Elite squad mates had made it into National squad, though. Camille had missed out due to injury, and Nancy . . . Ellie sighed at the thought of her best friend, who had given up gymnastics last year. Nancy's twin brother, Tam, was here with the boys' squad, but it wasn't quite the same as having Nancy herself here to share everything with.

'Welcome to National squad camp.' Ellie's thoughts were dragged sharply back to the present by the small, elegant, grey-haired figure of Barbara Steele, head national coach. She was addressing the twelve Junior girls who were lined up on the practice floor in their GB leotards, the Union Jack running across the shiny red fabric. Ellie had dreamed of wearing a GB leotard for her whole life and she still couldn't believe she'd finally earned the right to do so.

'I'll be overseeing all of the training camps taking place this week,' Barbara went on, looking them up and down critically, 'from the Seniors down to the babies who'll be arriving in a day or two.'

Ellie glanced over to where the Senior National squad were already warming up on the other side of the gym. She recognised Sian Edwards and Sophia Mitford, the two most senior gymnasts at the Academy, as well as a few other well-known faces. Just watching them made a shiver go down her spine. They had represented GB at the last Olympics, and Ellie dreamed of following in their footsteps one day. She could hardly believe she was training side by side with them now.

But Barbara's reference to the babies also made Ellie remember that most of the girls lined up alongside her had been coming to National squad camps since they were eight or nine years old. She was a late joiner – she had only arrived at the Academy last year – and so she had to prove she was as good as her squad mates.

'Your focus in this camp will be on new skills,' Barbara went on. 'You'll be working on new combination tumbles on the floor, more advanced vaults and acrobatics series on the beam, as well as new flight element combinations on the bars.'

Ellie felt a flicker of excitement. The last few months had been all about perfecting old skills. The opportunity to work on new manouevres was terrifying and thrilling at the same time.

4

'I want to see each of you stretching yourselves to the max,' said Barbara. 'I'll be looking for potential in this camp – I'm already thinking ahead to selections for European Championships later in the year.'

Ellie's heart started pounding again. Only five of the girls standing here today would be selected to go to Berlin for Euros. And looking at the others, she couldn't imagine she would be one of them. Apart from her old Academy squad mates – all of whom were stunning gymnasts – they were also up against Eva Reddle, the Junior British Champion, and her friend Willow Hall, both from the famous Liverpool gym. Then there were two incredibly talented Welsh gymnasts – Phoebe and Rosa – and a sweet little Irish girl called Niamh. And then there was Memory Danster.

Memory was the same age as Ellie but she looked much older. She was mid height with a tight, compact frame, broad shoulders and limbs so muscly they made Ellie's look like twigs that might snap at any minute. Even the expression on Memory's face was fierce. Her dark hair was tightly plaited to her scalp in cornrows which ran away from her furrowed brow, beneath which were a set of intense black eyes and a firmly-set mouth that looked as if it had forgotten how to smile.

Ellie had tried to say hello as they'd put their stuff in the lockers earlier, but Memory had completely blanked her.

'Perhaps she is just shy,' said serious, dark-haired Bella, who always tried to see the best in everyone.

'Or maybe she is getting out of bed on wrong side this morning,' said Katya. The tiny blonde-haired girl had grown up performing in a circus in Moscow, and she still spoke with a pronounced Russian accent. 'She will be friendly tomorrow.'

'Let's hope so,' said Ellie. From Memory's fierce expression, though, Ellie got the feeling that she wasn't here to make friends.

'I'll mainly be working with the Senior squad girls in the lead-up to Euros,' Barbara Steele was saying. Ellie tore her eyes away from Memory to focus on the head coach. 'But I am thrilled to announce that a brand-new coach will be overseeing the Junior GB squad.'

A shiver of excitement and anticipation rippled through the line of gymnasts. Katya turned to Ellie and mouthed, '*Lizzie?*'

Ellie's stomach did a flip. No, it couldn't be. Could it?

Lizzie Trengilly – Ellie's aunt – had been the greatest GB gymnast of all time, until her career had come to a tragic end when she was just eighteen, after a terrible fall at the Olympics.

'She is a name so familiar that she hardly needs an introduction,' Barbara went on. 'And she knows better than almost anyone what it takes to get to the top.'

Ellie's heart was racing. Could it be . . . could it be?

The thought of Lizzie being here – now – seemed both impossible and impossibly exciting! Ellie hadn't seen her for years. After her accident Lizzie had gone travelling round the world, barely sending more than the occasional postcard home. Ellie had always believed that Lizzie wasn't interested in her own gym career until the discovery a few months ago that her aunt had been watching all along. After that, Ellie's longing to see Lizzie – talk to her – get to know her – had deepened to a desperate ache.

'Ah, here she is . . .' said Barbara. 'Right on cue!'

Ellie heard the door to the gym swing open and the sound of footsteps crossing the mats. Her heart was pounding as she tried to catch a glimpse in the mirror, but she was standing at the wrong angle to see.

Could it be? Recently rumours had been circulating about Lizzie leaving her coaching job in California, about her returning to the the UK.

'Let me introduce . . . Vivian Ponting.'

Ellie turned round. There, striding across the blue floor in flip flops, was not Aunt Lizzie, but a taller gymnast, with broad shoulders, bleached blonde hair and a face so tanned her smile glowed whitely out of it.

'Hi guys!' the woman said, in a strong Australian drawl. 'It's grand to meet you all.'

Ellie's heart did a bellyflop. She felt a bitter pang of disappointment.

'Vivian is a vault expert,' Barbara was saying. 'She has an Olympic gold medal on vault, and she won all-around silver at World Champs as both a Junior and Senior gymnast, by performing some of the most difficult vaults ever seen in competition.'

As Ellie tried to push her disappointment to one side, she stared at the coach. Vivian's face looked familiar, although she couldn't quite place why.

'Vivian has been coaching in Australia,' Barbara went on, 'but she's kindly agreed to give up the sun and surf to help prepare you girls for Junior Europeans.'

Ellie knew she should be excited. They were lucky to be working with someone so experienced. She could teach them so much, and Ellie had come to National squad camp to learn. But all she could think was that Vivian wasn't Aunt Lizzie.

Vivian looked the line of gymnasts up and down critically. 'You'll hear a lot of people talking about the qualities that make great gymnasts,' she said in her lazy Australian drawl. 'Precision, technical skill, grace, artistry. These are all important.' Vivian's eyes narrowed as if she was weighing up each girl's potential in a single glance.

'But times are changing,' she went on. 'Nowadays great gymnastics, the kind of gymnastics you need to get to the top, requires power.' Her eyes came to rest on Memory for a second. 'I've no doubt you girls are bendy and graceful.' Vivian spoke dismissively as if none of that mattered. 'But to tackle new skills some of you are going to need to seriously build up your strength.'

Ellie glanced at herself in the mirror. She knew she was still short for her age, and compared to some of the others she was delicate. So were Bella and Katya. But she also knew all three of them possessed strength that might not be obvious.

'Strength protects you from injury,' Vivian went on. 'Torn muscles, ripped ligaments – all these are common in gymnastics because it's a high impact sport. The stronger you are, the less likely you are to sustain injuries.'

Ellie couldn't help thinking of Camille, out for a year with an ACL tear, and of Aunt Lizzie after her terrible fall at the Olympics; laid up in bed, her leg in plaster and all her hopes and dreams lying in tatters around her.

'So I'm going to build up your strength,' Vivian said. 'It's not going to be pretty – you're going to go to hell and back. But power comes from pain, that's what I say.'

Ellie knew that Nancy would have had something to say about Vivian's 'pain is power' mantra! She'd probably also have done a funny impression of the coach's Aussie accent which would have had them all in stitches. But maybe it was a good thing that Nancy wasn't there: Vivian didn't look like the type who would approve of giggling. She looked as though she didn't approve of much, in fact. Ellie had thought the Academy coaches were strict, but she had a feeling that Vivian would be ten times worse.

'Right, let's get to it!' said Vivian. 'The pain starts here, ladies!'

CHAPTER
Two

Ellie was right. She was used to gruelling conditioning sessions at the Academy, but this was worse than anything even the pre-Elite coach Oleg Petrescu could come up with. Back and forth across the floor they went – wheelbarrow walks, handstand walks, forward rolls, pikes to handstands, then forward rolls into back tucks. Over and over with no let-up whilst Vivian called out things like, 'No wiggling . . . you think you're a worm now? Keep those hips up, or do you need a hip replacement? Tuck your butt under . . . you ain't twerking now, ladies!'

'She's not big on compliments, is she?' asked

Bella breathlessly at the end of one set, looking at Ellie with a concerned expression on her face.

'She is a bossy-shoes, I think!' Katya managed to whisper.

'Bossy-boots!' giggled Ellie.

'Hey, Trengilly, stop gassing and let's step it up a gear!' Vivian yelled.

Ellie blushed and launched into a new series of continuous split leaps, pushing up off the ground to get as much height as possible.

'Open . . . open, Trengilly,' Vivian yelled. 'Come on, you're not even trying. You can get higher than that, can't you?'

Ellie gritted her teeth and dug even deeper. She'd always been incredibly good on flight work and she knew her split leaps had elevation and line that the other gymnasts envied, but all Vivian said at the end was, 'Shame you didn't point your toes.'

Ellie felt herself flush even brighter red. She was sure she had been pointing her toes the whole way through. She bit her lip and carried on with the next sequence, a forward roll into a back tuck.

Only Vivian wasn't finished with her.

'C'mon! You're not in the boxing ring, Ellie! . . . Point those toes! Tighter legs, tighter body, longer neck . . . higher, higher, higher!'

'Wow, she's got it in for you,' said Scarlett as the warm-up came to an end and the girls congregated round the lockers, glugging down water and pulling off their leggings ready for apparatus work.

Blonde and glamorous Scarlett had never been Ellie's greatest fan. Nancy called her 'Queen of Mean' and reckoned that Scarlett hated anyone with talent – which was probably why Ellie was top of her hit list! She certainly seemed to be enjoying watching Ellie squirm under Vivian's constant criticism now.

'What did you do to bug our new coach, I wonder?' said Kashvi, glancing at Ellie in concern. Kashvi stood with her hands on her hips, face creased into a frown.

'I guess not everyone is a fan of the name Trengilly,' said Scarlett, still smirking as she took a swig of water out of a pink jewel-encrusted bottle which bore the motto 'Star Gymnast'.

'What?' Ellie wanted Scarlett to explain what she had meant, but she'd already turned away. Vivian clapped her hands to hurry them all along.

'Come on, Trengilly,' she said. 'Less chit-chat and a bit more commitment to training.'

Ellie glanced around. Niamh and Rosa were still putting their water bottles away. Phoebe was looking for her guard bag and Bella and Kashvi were talking. Why was Vivian singling her out?

As they started apparatus work, things got worse. Ellie was put in a team with Eva, Memory, Scarlett and Katya. They were up on the vault first, which meant they were working with Vivian. She took them down to the pitted area, a side gym with high brick walls and a window looking out over the woods. It was filled with every kind of apparatus imaginable, sunk in large pits filled with foam logs.

'Like big soft cushions,' Katya sighed when she saw them. 'So we are not crackling any bones!'

'When you're working on new skills you want to work on soft surfaces,' Vivian told them. 'So, we'll

15

start out in the pit and safety mats now, then as we get closer to Euros we'll go back to competition surfaces.'

Ellie felt a flutter of excitement. If she could master a new vault with a higher difficulty value it could really raise her all-around score. Barbara Steele wanted to see potential – this could be Ellie's chance to show she had it.

'Will you teach us the Produnova?' asked Memory quietly. A slight American twang was mixed with her low Scottish burr. It was the first thing Ellie had heard her say all morning.

'Yes, that would be amazing!' said Eva, the tall, smiley-faced British Junior Champion. 'Only four people in the world can perform a Produnova.'

'Because it is super-dooper difficult,' said Katya.

'It carries a seven difficulty value,' muttered Memory, staring at the floor as she spoke.

'Nobody is learning the Produnova,' said Vivian sharply. 'It's a dangerous vault that should be banned.'

'But didn't you do it?' asked Scarlett. 'At

World Champs – *and* the Olympics.'

'And then I *stopped* performing it,' snapped Vivian, her tone of voice making it clear that this conversation was over.

'Can we at least work on Amanars?' asked Scarlett, a hint of a whine in her voice.

'Some of you don't yet have the power for the more complex vaults,' said Vivian, looking each of them up and down. 'Memory – you can try for an Amanar. Eva and Scarlett – I want to see you working towards two and a half Yurchenkos. Katya, I believe you are still a vault novice, so you and Ellie should stick to the single twist.'

'But . . .' Ellie started to say.

'You're lacking in the upper body strength for the more difficult vaults, Trengilly,' said Vivian firmly.

Ellie wanted to protest, to tell Vivian she was close to perfecting a *double* Yurchenko, but Vivian had already started walking away. 'Go measure up then we'll get started.'

'Wow, she doesn't leave much room for discussion, does she?' said Eva, seeing how disappointed Ellie

17

looked. 'Don't worry – when she sees how well you vault, she'll soon change her mind.'

Ellie smiled, hoping Eva was right.

Before they could begin, the girls had to measure their run ups and mark the start point with chalk. Then the springboard had to be carefully adjusted for each gymnast. The whole thing took a while.

Whilst they waited, Vivian made them do gruelling strength exercises. She had them hanging from the wooden bars set against the wall, pulling their feet to horizontal and down again. Vivian watched them all with eagle eyes, and Ellie was determined to prove she was just as strong as the others.

She held her own against the taller gymnasts in the workout, refusing to give in even when her muscles screamed in pain, but when they started vaulting it was hard not to be impressed by the strength of girls like Memory and Eva. Eva was famous for her beautiful vaulting that made her seem almost as if she was flying, and Memory was so powerful that she seemed to explode into the air like a rocket.

'Wow, she has got vaulting va-va-voom!' said

Katya, her face so serious as she pronounced this that Ellie struggled not to burst into giggles. But Katya was right. Eva Reddle had won vault gold at the British this year, but Memory, who'd been training in the US for the past three years, was in a class above even her. When it came to Ellie's turn she was already feeling seriously under pressure. She wanted to prove to Vivian that they'd got off on the wrong foot.

'Show me a single Yurchenko, Trengilly,' snapped Vivian as Ellie stepped up to the runway.

But Ellie had already decided what she was going to do. She took the vault run up at full speed, hit the springboard with as much force as she could muster and flung herself up, pushing off the vault and twisting, once . . . one and a half times . . . twice in the air. She'd under-rotated slightly so she had to pull herself sharply back on landing, forcing her foot down so hard to prevent herself toppling that she felt a jolt of pain shoot up her ankle. She took a step back but somehow remained upright. Then, determined not to show weakness in front of her

19

new coach, she took a deep breath and turned to Vivian with a smile.

The coach did not smile back. 'Did I tell you to chuck a double, Trengilly?'

'I . . . I just thought . . .' Ellie stammered, trying to ignore the throbbing pain in her ankle. 'I had the speed so I . . . I thought I'd try for the double twist.'

'Yeah, well, your take-off isn't high enough yet,' said Vivian, 'and you're not aggressive enough in your push to land a double safely.'

'But I thought that . . .'

'You're also pulling your shoulder back too early,' Vivian went on, her face unyielding. 'You shouldn't allow your feet to go over your hands till your body is starting to bend . . .'

'Right, I . . .'

'*Right.*' Vivian glared at her. 'So until you can get all that correct, I want you to stick to singles – nothing more than a one and half till I say so. Get it?'

Ellie was struggling with a mixture of emotions – disappointment, embarrassment, anger – and the horrible shooting pain in her ankle. She struggled to keep her voice even as she said, 'But I thought we were working up new skills . . .'

Vivian stuck her hands on her hips and narrowed her eyes. 'Trengilly, you wanna remember who the coach is here?'

Ellie bit her lip hard.

'Come back to me when you've got a bit more muscle in those scrawny arms and then we'll talk about upgrades!'

Ellie turned away, her eyes blurry with tears, her face burning with humiliation and her ankle throbbing. It had been just about the worst start to her week at National squad camp possible.

Luckily, the rest of the session went a bit better. Bar, beam and floor with the other coaches was hard work but Ellie found working on new skills exhilarating. She received as much encouragement as critique, even if her ankle did continue to bother her throughout the session. She was by far the strongest on bars – where not even Memory could match her difficulty value – and on floor and beam her artistry was scored as highly as her power tumbles and acro sequences.

The other coaches seemed keen to help her upgrade, and it was a relief to find that not everyone thought she was a completely hopeless gymnast. But Ellie knew that if she was to get a look-in for the Euros squad – or even get a call-back for the selection weekend in six weeks' time – she was going to have to impress Vivian – or be left out in the cold.

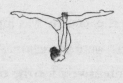

CHAPTER
Three

'Vivian's totally got it in for me,' Ellie told Tam when they sat down for supper that night. At the heart of the National Sports Training Centre was a beautiful old honey-coloured mansion, which housed the dining hall and the dorms where the gymnasts slept during their week at camp. Surrounding this were a collection of state-of-the-art sports facilities, medical centres, and physio and rehab units. Beyond them were formal gardens and then sports pitches and training grounds for every sport under the sun.

Athletes and sportspeople from every discipline came here to train ahead of international events, but right now the centre was pretty empty; the only people there were the gymnasts who would be training there intensively for the next seven days – eating, sleeping and breathing gymnastics!

The food in the canteen was delicious, although Ellie found she had lost her appetite.

'Maybe it's not you she's annoyed at,' suggested Tam, who had definitely not lost his. He was tucking into a giant bowl of sticky toffee pudding as if he hadn't eaten for days.

Tam had detached himself from the other Junior boys to come and join the girls from the Academy, who were all sitting together. Even the Senior squad girls Sian Edwards and Sophia Mitford had come to keep the younger girls company. Tam was the only boy from the Academy who'd qualified for GB squad this year. Olympic medallist Matt Simmons was out with an injury and Tam's Academy squad mate Robbie had performed poorly at the British so missed out on selection. But this didn't seem to bother Tam. He'd been coming to squad camps since he was a kid – this was his fifth time here, so he knew lots of the boys from other clubs. Ellie was glad he made time to see them during mealtimes.

'I feel like I've done something to annoy Vivian,' she said. 'But I have no idea what!'

'That's not hard to work out,' Tam went on, wiping toffee sauce off his chin with a shrug. 'Everyone knows she and Lizzie were deadly rivals.'

'*Were* they?' said Ellie.

'Ellie, sometimes I think you know nothing about gymnastic history at all!' said Bella, shaking her head in disbelief.

'You really don't!' Sian laughed. 'It's one of the most famous rivalries in gym history!'

'Lizzie and Vivian were rivals?' Ellie repeated. How did everyone else know this and not her?

'Even I know this!' said Katya, shaking her head as if reading her thoughts.

'Oh,' said Ellie. 'Right.'

'What *do* you actually know about Vivian Ponting?' asked Sian gently. She might be an Olympic gold medallist, but kind Sian always

25

had time for the younger gymnasts.

'Not much,' Ellie admitted.

'OK, let's start from the beginning,' said Tam, grinning at Ellie. Things had been a bit weird between them earlier in the year. Robbie had teased Tam about being Ellie's boyfriend and for a while they hadn't really spoken. But now they were back to normal again, and Ellie was glad – she'd missed him and his sense of humour. 'So, Vivian was known for her bubbly personality, OK?'

'She was always chatting to the TV cameras mid-competition,' agreed Kashvi. 'High-fiving judges, disco dancing after a great score.'

'Writing messages on her palm and holding them up on the podium,' added Tam. 'She was cool!'

Ellie tried to imagine it. Strict Vivian being funny and cool, and messing around? Wow!

'But she was deadly serious as a competitor,' said Sian. 'Incredibly ambitious. She always said she wanted to get to the top, no matter what it took.'

'There was only one thing standing in her way,' said Kashvi. 'And that was . . .'

'Lizzie Trengilly!' said Katya and Tam at exactly the same time.

'I see,' said Ellie. It was all starting to make sense now.

'The reason Vivian Ponting has so many *silver* medals is because Lizzie beat her into second place in everything,' explained Sian.

'But she won Olympic gold,' said Ellie.

'The year Lizzie injured herself and had to pull out,' Bella finished for her.

Ellie was silent for a moment, taking it all in. She'd spent hours, poring over pictures of Aunt Lizzie, but she'd never paid much attention to her competitors. But of course that's why Vivian had looked familiar – she'd seen her dozens of times, standing on podiums next to Lizzie. Always on her left, the silver medal spot.

'Vivian was a huge talent. In any other era she'd have been the greatest gymnast in the world,' said Sian. 'But because of Lizzie she was always the runner-up.'

Ellie glanced over to where Vivian was sitting

27

with Barbara Steele and the boys' coaches. She wondered how that had felt – always finding herself in second place. Never quite good enough to win the gold. Was she still mad about it? Was that why she disliked Ellie?

'After Lizzie retired, Vivian kept competing for a bit, but she was never as good,' said Sian, ruefully. 'It was almost like . . . like she lost her edge when she stopped chasing Lizzie.'

'I don't think she ever won a major gold medal after that, did she?' said Tam.

Sian shook her head. 'She's quite a lot older than your aunt,' she said. 'Lizzie was only eighteen when she retired, but Vivian was at least twenty-five by then. Other younger gymnasts came along and Vivian dropped down the ranks.'

'She retired a couple of years after Lizzie's injury,' Bella added.

'Vivian doesn't like me because of my aunt!' Ellie said with despair. What could she do to change that?

'At least it makes a change from you getting the star treatment all the time,' said Scarlett who was walking past arm in arm with the sweet, fluffy-haired Welsh girl, Phoebe. 'If you live by the sword you die by the sword, I say!'

'Which means what, exactly?' demanded Tam.

'Just that Ellie gets all the perks of the Trengilly name,' said Scarlett. 'So it's only fair she should cope with the downsides too!'

'Scarlett, Ellie's got this far on her own talent,' said Sian firmly. 'Nothing to do with Lizzie. We all know that.'

'Do we?' said Scarlett sulkily. She looked as if she wanted to say more, but even she didn't dare when Sian was there.

'Yes, we do,' said Sian firmly. 'And I'm also sure that Vivian is far too professional to punish Ellie for her family connection.'

Kashvi looked doubtful. 'She is being super mean to Ellie though.'

'I expect she just wants to push you,' said Sian, although even she didn't sound completely convinced. 'She does it to everyone.'

'Well, I'm just saying I wouldn't want to be

training a relative of my deadly enemy,' said Scarlett.

'Lucky that most human beings are lot nicer than you then, isn't it!' muttered Tam as Scarlett turned away with a flick of her blonde mane, dragging a rather reluctant Phoebe along with her.

'There's nothing I can do about it,' said Ellie. 'It's not like I can stop being Lizzie's niece, can I?'

'Just keep working on your own programme,' said Sian. 'She'll see how great you are.'

Ellie sighed. At least now she knew the reason why Vivian seemed to have it in for her. She just didn't know how to fix it!

CHAPTER
Four

Ellie sat on the edge of the bath with an ice pack pressed against her ankle, her eyes squeezed shut. The pain in her ankle seemed to have got worse as the day went on and as she glanced down at it she saw it was red and swollen. She hadn't told anyone it was bothering her. There was no point, she told herself. It would be better by tomorrow.

'Ellie, come on!' she heard Tam call. 'Nancy and Lucy want to talk to you.'

'Coming!' said Ellie, hastily stuffing the ice pack in her wash bag and strapping up her foot to hide the bruising. She didn't want the others to make a fuss.

'Seriously, how long do you girls take in the bathroom?' said Tam when she emerged a few minutes later. He was lounging in a chair in the neat little double room that Katya and Ellie were sharing for the week.

'How did you even get in here?' she asked, trying to change the subject. 'I thought boys weren't allowed in the girls' dorms.'

'Oh, I just told the coaches you were Skyping my sister and they said it was cool.' Tam grinned. 'And now I've discovered that you girls have a secret stash of cake I'll be over every day to help you eat it!' He waved a slice of home-made flapjack in the air.

'Um, what happened to the food Mandy packed for you?' asked Ellie. Mandy was the housemother who looked after the Academy gymnasts back in Head-Over-Heels House, their boarding house in London. She was also Tam and Nancy's mum – and an amazing cook.

'Oh, I got peckish on the journey up!' said Tam, his mouth full of syrup and oats. 'What took you so long in there anyway?'

'I was just – doing a . . . face pack,' Ellie lied, unconvincingly. Tam raised his eyebrow, but fortunately just then Katya yelped and pointed at the laptop propped up on her bed. Nancy and Lucy were waving at them on the screen from the bedroom they shared in Trengilly Cottage.

Since Nancy had given up gym for good less than a year ago, she lived in Cornwall with Ellie's family and shared a bedroom with Ellie's gym-mad little sister, Lucy. Nancy was crazy about anything to do with boats and now that she had swapped somersaults for rowing, she seemed happier than she'd ever been.

'Vivian Ponting – you're kidding. She was a real laugh as a competitor, wasn't she?' asked Nancy, when Tam had filled her in on the day's events.

'Not these days she isn't,' said Ellie, curling up on the bed next to Katya, tucking her strapped ankle out of sight. 'The only jokes she cracks are about how bad everything I do is! Trust me, you're missing nothing.'

'Oh – I'm not missing gymnastics at all,' said

Nancy cheerfully. 'I'm so totally over all that. It's all about the pilot gig championships. That's where it's happening. Trust me!'

'Pilot gig?' asked Tam, pulling a face.

'Bro, you never listen to anything I tell you!' said Nancy. 'Pilot gigs are six-man rowing boats. They were originally designed to ferry pilots out to sailing ships to help them navigate around the Cornish coastline.'

'Sometimes they were used as lifeboats too,' added Lucy, helpfully. Ellie's little sister was like a smaller, red-haired version of Ellie herself. Ellie had missed her like mad when she first went to the Academy – she still did, although she was happier leaving Lucy now that Nancy was there, like a second big sister.

'Yup, but now they just race for fun,' Nancy went on. 'There are loads of events coming up.'

'I wonder if we'll get to come and watch you,' said Ellie. She hadn't been back to Cornwall since Christmas and she was more homesick than she could admit.

'Ooh, yes – this will be good!' said Katya. She

had struck up a firm friendship with Lucy last time they'd all been to stay, over Christmas. Her own family were far away in the Russian circus, so she'd been half-adopted by Ellie's family too.

'Ok, so after you guys win your golds at Euros you can chill by the seaside and watch me do the same,' said Nancy.

'Sounds perfect!' said Ellie, with a sigh. 'Only I'm not sure I'll be making it to Euros if Vivian has any say in the matter.'

CHAPTER
Five

The next morning's warm-up went a lot like the previous one, with Vivian finding fault with almost everything Ellie did.

'Your arms are too wide, Trengilly . . . tuck your bum under – you look like a duck there . . . lift your feet up – are you wearing a pair of welly boots, Trengilly?'

Ellie found it hard to concentrate. She was constantly being reminded what she was getting wrong. It didn't help that her foot was in more pain than ever this morning. Even walking on it made her wince, but she still hadn't mentioned it to anyone.

Luckily, the others were all too immersed in their own training to notice. Only Scarlett picked up on the strained look on Ellie's face. 'Can't take the pace?' she enquired nastily.

'No, I'm fine,' said Ellie. 'Never been better!'

'A week at National squad camp is a test of endurance,' said Scarlett with a silky smile. 'Only the fittest survive!'

'Bring it on!' said Ellie. She tried to sound brave, but Scarlett had a curious expression on her face as she turned away.

After warm-up, Ellie was on tumble track, working on new tumble combinations. Even the *thought* of landing hard on her ankle made her feel sick, but when Barbara Steele wandered over to where the Juniors were working, Ellie pushed the pain to the back of her mind, determined to impress the head national coach.

She delivered a round-off double back straight, landing easily on the safety mat, ignoring the screaming pain that shot through her ankle on impact.

'What else are you working on?'

Ellie turned and saw that Barbara Steele was talking to her.

'Oh – um – I'm trying to master a double back straight into front punch,' said Ellie, hoping her eyes did not betray the pain that was still making it hard to think straight. 'I'm nearly there.'

'Let's see it, then.'

Ellie took a deep breath and tried not to hobble as she made her way back to the far end of the tumble track. Vivian had come to join Barbara and was saying something to the head coach. She waited for the signal to go, rotating her ankle to try and shake off the throbbing pain.

'Is that foot bothering you, Trengilly?' asked Vivian, looking up sharply.

'No . . . it's just . . . I bashed it earlier. On the bars.'

'You need it checked out in the medical centre?'

'It's fine. I just need an ice pack.'

'After you finish here you get it looked at, OK?' said Vivian curtly. 'Now, show us what you've got.'

Ellie powered into the tumble – more self-conscious now that Vivian was watching. She rotated neatly through the air and landed it with only a slight stumble, feeling her ankle jar agonisingly but planting it firmly and refusing to wobble.

'Good effort,' said Barbara with a nod.

'Your arms are still too wide on take-off,' said Vivian. 'And I'd still like to see more directional change. Here.'

She walked over to Ellie, who was still reeling slightly from the pain, stood behind her and lifted her arms up in the air. 'Like this.' Vivian slowly rotated Ellie's body, mimicking the position she needed to achieve in the air. 'Pull your shoulders right back and lift your chest up – it'll help you power through.'

Ellie nodded. What Vivian said made sense, but she was feeling slightly dizzy, and she was unable to relax in Vivian's presence after all she'd learned about her past the previous day.

'Try again,' said Vivian sharply, glancing at Ellie's bound foot as she walked back to the start of the track, doing her very best not to limp.

This time Ellie took the tumble recalling all that Vivian had said, and she landed it tightly, ignoring the shot of pain on landing.

'Not bad, I suppose,' was all Vivian had to say. 'Now go see the doc about that ankle, Trengilly.' Then she turned and walked away.

Ellie made her way over to the medical centre, feeling weirdly tearful. Vivian's eye for detail was incredible. Ellie knew she could learn so much from her – if only Vivian was willing to teach her!

The doctor, Sam, was a tall guy with dreadlocks and a Cockney accent.

'So, what's bothering you, missus?' he asked, with a white toothy grin.

'Nothing much,' said Ellie. The pain had receded a little and the lie came easily. 'I just bashed my ankle this morning on the bar. I guess I need a bag of ice to hold against it or something.'

'Can I take a look?'

Ellie reluctantly hopped up on the table and allowed Sam to examine her ankle. He rotated it this way and that and asked her to point and stretch her toes several times.

'You sure you just bashed it?' he asked, looking up at her with a serious expression in his eyes. 'Nothing more than that?'

'Nope,' Ellie shook her head, although she could feel herself blushing.

'It's important that you're completely honest,' said Sam. 'Something that starts out as a niggle can turn into a progressive injury if left untreated.'

'I know,' said Ellie, forcing herself to meet his eye. 'But it's nothing. I just caught it – that's all.'

Sam finally gave a shrug. 'OK – I can't feel anything wrong. I'm going to give you an ice pack, and I want to keep an eye on it so I'll need you back here tomorrow, OK?'

Ellie nodded.

'If it doesn't get better you need to rest it,' Sam went on. 'Give it time to recover. Your body is like a machine, you have to look after it or it will malfunction.'

'I know,' said Ellie, her face flushing again. The

knot of anxiety in her stomach suddenly hurt as much as her foot. Keeping the pain secret was agony too, and part of her wanted to blurt out the whole story to someone. But she had no choice. If she told Sam how much it hurt, he'd say she had to stop training, and that just wasn't an option right now.

'There's really nothing wrong with me,' she insisted, biting her lip hard to keep back the tears. 'I promise.'

CHAPTER
Six

'We figured it out,' said Lucy when Ellie Skyped them again that evening. Lucy, who was crazy about gymnastics, had made Ellie and Katya promise to give her daily National squad camp updates. Ellie didn't mind – she always loved hearing what was going on back home in Cornwall in exchange.

'Yup, we know why Vivian's being so mean to you!' said Nancy. Her freckled face was looking brown as a nut and she was grinning happily out of the screen, like she'd just solved a big mystery.

'We know!' said Ellie. 'She didn't like Aunt Lizzie!'

'No, it's more than that,' said Lucy. 'She's

43

stopping you trying the hard stuff, right?'

'Yes,' Ellie admitted. 'I don't even care about her being harsh but I just feel like she's deliberately holding me back – especially on vault.'

'And that completely makes sense,' said Nancy, triumphantly.

'Um – why?' said Ellie. 'Explain.'

'So we've been reading all about her in this biography,' Lucy held up a copy of a book. It was called *Silver Linings – an Unauthorised Biography of Vivian Ponting*, and it had a picture of a young Vivian on the front, her face screwed up in concentration as she sailed over the vault.

'Wow!' said Katya, who was sitting in the splits on the floor as if it was the most natural position in the world. 'Lucy, you are doing detective work!' she squeaked, grinning at her pal who smiled back happily.

'Lizzie was beating Vivian in every competition,' said Lucy. 'So when it came to World Champs, Vivian decided she needed to do something drastic to beat her.'

'What did she do?' asked Katya, who had levered herself up into an elephant lift and was talking to the screen from her upside-down position.

'That's when she decided to attempt the Produnova vault,' said Nancy.

'Whoa!' said Tam. He appeared in the doorway and flung himself down on the bed. He was now a regular feature in the girls' dorms, which he had announced were far more comfortable – and less smelly – than the boys'. Some of the Junior squad boys had started calling him a ladies' man, but Ellie figured his visits had more to do with their cake! 'Sorry I'm late – what did I miss?'

'Just shut up and listen!' said Nancy, although Ellie saw her grin, and knew she was pleased to see him really.

'Love you too, big sis!' said Tam, blowing her a mock kiss.

'Yuk,' said Nancy, pretending to wipe it off her chin. 'Now where was I?'

'The Produnova.'

'Oh, yes,' said Nancy. She boomed out in a

dramatic voice over. 'Everyone knows that the Produnova is the most difficult vault there is!'

'And fiendishly dangerous!' Lucy chipped in, not quite getting her voice right and giggling. 'But Vivian knew it would give her such a high difficulty value that Lizzie would struggle to beat it – *if* she could nail it.'

'I think I remember reading something about this,' said Tam, who was now munching on a stash of muffins he'd found in Ellie's suitcase. The fact that they'd eaten a giant meal less than half an hour earlier didn't seem to make any difference to him; as usual, he was already starving. 'It was a massive controversy in the end – right?'

'What happened?' asked Ellie. She knew her aunt had won gold at World Champs.

'Well, Vivian did the Produnova,' said Lucy. 'But she stumbled in her landing, so she lost execution points.'

'Which meant that she and Lizzie ended up with exactly the same all-around score,' said Nancy.

'Exactly the same?' said Ellie.

'That is very unusual,' said Katya, who was now the right way up again.

'Completely!' said Nancy. 'It hardly ever happens, and it was a massive deal – it meant a tie for gold medal at World Champs.'

'So they shared gold medal?' asked Katya.

'Nope!' said Nancy. 'Lizzie got it.'

'Of course,' said Tam. 'Lizzie won, because execution score trumps difficulty value score, right?'

'Right,' said Nancy. 'Even though their total was the same, the judges awarded the gold to Lizzie.'

'So the difficulty of Vivian's Produnova vault didn't help?' said Ellie, trying to figure out exactly what this meant. 'She still came second.'

'And that's why she won't let you try difficult vaults!' said Lucy.

'She's punishing you for what Lizzie did to her all those years ago,' added Nancy.

Ellie felt dismayed. She recalled Vivian's refusal to let Ellie even try another vault, her constant nit-picking of Ellie's technique.

'You two are like Sherlock Holmes and Dr

47

Watson, aren't you?' said Tam, who had just polished off his third muffin. 'Super gym-sleuths in search of the truth!'

'We had to work out what Vivian is doing. We can't let her ruin Ellie's chances cos of some ancient grudge against Lizzie!' said Nancy.

'So, what can I do?' said Ellie.

'I've got an idea,' said Tam.

CHAPTER
Seven

'OK, this is top secret, right?' said Tam, as he and Ellie made their way across the darkened lawns the following evening. 'Cos we're not the only ones who'll get in trouble if we're found out.'

'I understand,' Ellie whispered, glancing around nervously. She'd noticed the rehabilitation centre when she'd arrived at the National Sports Training Centre. It was a modern building on the other side of the campus which housed state-of-the-art physiotherapy facilities for injured soldiers.

'I spoke to one of the squaddies and he promised to leave a window open,' Tam went on. 'But he'll be in big trouble with his unit commander if we get caught.'

'How come he's even helping us?' asked Ellie.

'His sister's a mad-keen gymnast,' Tam explained, checking that the coast was clear before sidling round the back of the rehabilitation centre building. 'And he used to be pretty good himself before . . . you know.'

Ellie nodded. Over the past few days she'd seen quite a few injured soldiers on the campus, on crutches or in wheelchairs. She found the idea of life after a war injury hard to even imagine. It made her ankle – which seemed to be getting worse rather than better – seem trivial in comparison. Not that she'd mentioned the getting-worse bit to Sam when she'd gone for her daily check up earlier, of course.

'Here we are,' said Tam, pushing himself through a bush to a low window that was half open. 'He said he'd leave the window on the catch so we can climb in. Give me a leg up.'

Ellie glanced around nervously. Tam's secret training session idea was brilliant, but it was also totally against the rules. If anyone saw them using equipment unsupervised – let alone breaking into a facility after lights-out – it would mean instant dismissal from camp, and probably from National squad, for both of them. Tam was making light of it, but Ellie knew he was risking a lot for her sake.

She remembered how she'd once thought she'd lost Tam's friendship forever, when Robbie had been teasing him about being her boyfriend. She'd missed him like mad then, but she realised now that she never could have lost him. He was a true friend.

But this was no time to start getting soppy. Tam hoiked Ellie up after him and she peered inside the open window. 'Wow – there's a fully equipped gym in here.' She wasn't sure what she'd expected, but it wasn't this.

'Get a move on!' whispered Tam.

Ellie managed to clamber in, then she grabbed Tam's arm and dragged him over the sill, toppling him over so that he landed with a crash on top of her.

'Ow . . . geroff! Do you mind?' he cried.

They both dissolved into giggles.

51

'You have no idea how much grief I'd get if the other boys could see me now!' laughed Tam. Ellie shoved him off and they both jumped to their feet. Ellie could feel herself flushing, and for a moment she couldn't look him in the eye. It was pretty dark in the unlit gym. Only the light of the street lamps flooded in through the high windows, but in it she could make out ropes and parallel bars, a vault and a tumble track, plus lots of other unfamiliar equipment which Ellie supposed must be for the soldiers' physio sessions.

'I reckon we've got an hour before lights-out,' said Tam. 'So get vaulting, Trengilly. The gym is all yours.'

Ellie suddenly felt nervous. The vault here didn't have a pit, so landing was going to be agony. 'You can do a double Yurchenko, right?' she asked Tam.

Tam nodded. 'Actually, I can do an Amanar,' he admitted modestly.

'Wow!' said Ellie, although she didn't know why she was surprised. Tam had won gold at British Champs – he was a dead cert for the boys' Euros squad. Of course he could nail the Amanar!

'So – um – maybe you can give me some tips?' Ellie asked. She couldn't quite shake off the shyness that had suddenly come over her now that it was just her and Tam, alone in the dark.

But Tam was businesslike. 'Love to!' he grinned. 'I've always fancied myself as a coach. Do I need to make you do a gruelling warm-up first?'

'Don't get carried away!' laughed Ellie, pushing aside her awkwardness and focusing on what they'd come for.

'Pain is power, Trengilly!' Tam whispered in a fake Aussie accent that had them both doubled up.

It turned out Tam was a great coach with a fantastic eye for detail. 'Nice and square . . . keep your kneecaps tight . . . make your take-off higher . . . better.'

Ellie was soon landing the double confidently. It hurt like mad and she was glad it was too dark in the gym for Tam to see the pained expression in her eyes. She was pretty sure he'd try to stop her if he knew how much she was hurting. 'I want to try for an Amanar,' she said.

Tam squinted at her through the gloom. 'You realise that needs a more powerful take-off?'

'You sound like Vivian again,' said Ellie.

'Fine,' said Tam with a slight frown on his face. It made Ellie wonder if he had spotted that something wasn't quite right. 'You need to be aggressive, then – punch the vault really hard – then plant your feet in the landing like you're trying to make a hole in the floor.'

Ellie swallowed. Her foot was throbbing again, but she couldn't think about that right now. Ignoring the pain, she took a deep breath and started into the run up. But then she spooked, stopping just short of the vault and crashing into it with a thud.

'You OK?' asked Tam, running over to where Ellie stood, breathless and winded.

'I'm fine,' said Ellie, not looking him in the eye. 'I just thought I heard something – someone coming.' It was a lie – she'd spooked because her foot was aching – but at that moment they actually did hear footsteps and voices outside the window. They both stopped silent for a moment and listened breathlessly. After a moment the sounds retreated into the background.

'We'd better not stay too much longer,' whispered Tam, his eyes running over her face as if he was trying to figure something out. 'Try it again. This time imagining you're punching Vivian when you smack into that vault.'

Ellie managed a quiet laugh as she made her way back to the beginning of the runway. Determined not to spook again, she tried to push all thoughts of her ankle out of her brain as she ran up. She hit the vault hard and twisted, once, twice . . . but this time something made her pull back at the last moment and she landed on her bum.

They tried the vault over and over and a couple of times Ellie planted it, but mostly she ended up toppling on to her bottom, or falling flat on her face. She was really struggling to push aside the pain and focus on the vault. She knew that was making her hold back.

'Perhaps we should stop for tonight?' suggested Tam.

'No,' Ellie insisted. 'I need to get it.' The gym was too dark for him to see her flushed face, but she looked away anyway.

'I'm just saying – sometimes you need to take a break and then come back to it fresh.'

'I don't have time to take a break!' Ellie said, louder than she intended. 'I need to nail this by the end of camp.'

'OK, OK, don't get your leotard in a twist!' Then he stopped. 'What was that?'

A light had come on just down the corridor and they could hear voices not far off – two female voices. 'Training in secret . . .' said someone Ellie didn't know. There were some unintelligible words, then, 'sneaking around . . . recovering from injury.' Then they heard the other person speak, in a voice with a familiar Australian twang to it.

'It's Vivian,' she whispered to Tam. They were both crouched down behind the vault in the dark. Ellie could hear Tam's heart beating and was sure her own was just as loud. She suddenly felt like he was too close.

'Perhaps someone told her we're here?' she whispered.

'We need to get out quick!' said Tam. 'Come on.'

They raced to the window, the voices getting closer as they did so. Ellie caught a fragment of the first voice: '. . . going behind everyone's backs . . .' Vivian replied something about 'punishment' and then they both laughed.

Tam put out a hand to lift Ellie up, but she stepped back.

'You go first,' she told him. 'I can't risk you being caught for me.'

Everything felt weird. Being here alone with Tam. Lying to him about her ankle. Not being able to look him in the eye.

'Nope – ladies first,' Tam insisted. 'No one can say I'm not a gentleman.'

Ellie hesitated, the pain making her feel dizzy and more confused than ever. A door slammed and the footsteps came closer.

'Come on, Ellie,' Tam urged. 'Or we'll both be caught.'

So Ellie allowed Tam to push her up over the sill. She landed in the bushes and fell awkwardly on her foot as she descended. She almost screamed out in pain but managed to muffle it. A moment later she was up and pulling Tam out too.

'Come on!' said Tam again, grabbing her hand as the light in the gym went on. They both legged it through the bushes back towards the dormitories. Glancing up at the clock tower, Ellie saw it was already past ten. They should have been in bed over an hour ago. The coaches didn't come round checking; they trusted that none of the gymnasts would be stupid enough to blow their chance by breaking the rules. But they slept in rooms just along the corridor from the gymnasts, and if Ellie and Tam were caught . . .

Ellie's ankle was in agony and she knew her body was covered in scratches from landing in the bush. And as they snuck back into the boarding house – red-faced and out of breath – they bumped into the tall, quiet figure of Memory Danster, making her way from the shared girls' kitchen area with a mug of hot chocolate in her hands, wrapped in a giant dressing gown.

Ellie and Tam came to a breathless halt. 'Hi,' they both said at once.

Ellie knew they must look totally suspicious. Back past curfew, red-faced and covered in leaves.

But all Memory said was a gruff, 'Hi.' She didn't ask where they'd been or what they'd been up to. She just shuffled past them and made her way back to her room.

'Has anyone ever heard that girl say more than a single word?' asked Tam.

'Well, let's hope she doesn't say anything to Vivian,' said Ellie, a thrill of fear pulsing through her stomach. 'Or we're both going home!'

CHAPTER
Eight

But they weren't caught. In fact, the next two days went much like the previous two, with Ellie in more and more pain – but having to lie to Sam about it – and constantly in the firing line from Vivian who seemed to find more fault with her each session. Sometimes Ellie found herself longing for the week to end so she could go back to the Academy, back to coaches who tried to see the best in her. But at other times, she felt the days were slipping by too fast, that she was running out of time to prove to the GB coaches she had potential.

Scarlett was loving every minute of Ellie's ordeal.

'Did you hear what Vivian said about my beam work this morning? I think her exact words were, "Gorgeous, gorgeous!"'

'Yeah, but weren't her next words, "And now you need to upgrade your skills if you want to make it to the Euros selection weekend"?' asked Kashvi, winking at Bella.

Scarlett coloured. 'At least she considers me capable of tackling new skills,' she snapped back. 'Ellie's still doing vaults I was doing when I was ten.'

Ellie tried not to let Scarlett's comments get to her, but it was hard enough being in pain and keeping it secret without having Vivian on her back all the time. She needed to make a good impression if she wanted to get a call-back for the Euros selections in six weeks' time, but Vivian seemed determined to see the worst in her. If it hadn't been for Tam's secret coaching sessions she'd have been totally in despair by the second-last day.

'I still can't believe you're letting my baby bro tell you what to do,' said Nancy when they Skyped that evening. She was dressed in a giant old fisherman's jumper and a hat that said 'First mate' on it. She was lounging in a battered armchair in the kitchen of Trengilly Cottage, looking so comfortable that Ellie couldn't help feeling a twinge of homesickness.

'Hey – less of the baby!' said Tam. 'I was born exactly three minutes after you.'

'And you're about three feet shorter than me!' grinned Nancy. 'Which makes you my ickle lickle brother!'

'He's actually really good!' said Ellie loyally. It was true. She'd had two more secret sessions with Tam and, even though the weird awkward thing continued to linger between them, Ellie was now really close to nailing the Amanar. And that was all thanks to Tam's coaching.

'You hear that, sis?' said Tam. 'At least someone appreciates me!'

Nancy just pulled a face.

'I still wish Lizzie were our coach instead of Vivian!' chipped in Katya, who was busy packing her case, getting ready for their return to London the next day.

'Talking of Lizzie, have you guys back home heard any more about what she's up to?' asked Tam.

'Ooh, yes,' said Ellie. Nancy and Lucy had promised to ask Dad about Lizzie and Ellie was surprised how desperate she was to know what they'd found out. 'Did you speak to Dad about it?'

'Yes – and he definitely knows what's going on!' said Lucy.

Ellie had found herself thinking about her aunt a lot this week. Maybe it was being at National squad camp, maybe it was the nagging anxiety about her injury, but she wished so much that her aunt was around for her to talk to.

'And what is going on?' asked Tam.

'That's the thing – he won't tell us!' said Nancy, screwing up her face crossly. 'He just tapped his nose and looked all mysterious and said we'd know soon enough. It was maddening!'

'Didn't he tell you *anything*?' asked Ellie, disappointed and more desperate to know than ever.

'Nope!' said Nancy. 'But I overheard him talking

to your mum the other day, Ellie. He was saying something about Lizzie and the Academy. He shut up pretty quickly when he realised I was listening, but I wonder . . .'

'Maybe that's it!' said Ellie, a flicker of hope flashing through her mind. 'She's not coaching here – but she'll be at the Academy. Wouldn't that be awesome? When we leave here tomorrow and go back to London, we'll find Lizzie there waiting for us.' She sighed dreamily at the thought of having a coach who was on her side, rather than out to get her.

'I guess we'll find out soon enough,' said Tam. 'We'll be back at Head-Over-Heels House tomorrow night!'

'I don't know about you, but I'm really looking forward to getting back to London,' said Ellie, thinking longingly of the rambling old boarding house the gymnasts all called home whilst at the Academy. 'I mean, I was so excited about this camp, and it has been amazing, but . . .'

'But it'll be nice not to be picked on in training

every day, right?' said Nancy, who knew Ellie almost better than anyone. She seemed to even be able to read her mind over Skype.

Ellie nodded. 'Right.'

The truth was that Ellie's first National squad camp hadn't gone as she'd imagined at all. She'd arrived with such high hopes, but Vivian had squashed them out of her. And though she'd expected to make new friends, apart from Eva Reddle, the other Junior girls hadn't been very friendly. Memory Danster, especially, had seemed in a permanent bad mood, and Scarlett was more fiercely competitive than ever. Ellie supposed it was because they were all so focused on impressing the coaches, but it still seemed a shame that there wasn't more team spirit.

'Yeah, and spending night after night hiding out in a dark gym with Tam!' said Nancy. 'I mean, yuk!'

'It's what most girls dream of!' said Tam with a shrug.

'Yeah, right!' said Nancy. 'It's enough to give any girl nightmares, don't you mean?!'

'Isn't it time you went off and found a boat to mess around in?' asked Tam. 'Ellie and I have an important training session to get to! We've got to make sure she can land that Amanar before camp is over so she'll get a call-back for the Euros selection weekend, don't you know!'

CHAPTER
Nine

Ellie woke the next morning feeling slightly sick. She hadn't slept well. The pain in her foot had kept her tossing and turning – and when she'd finally drifted off, her sleep had been fitful and full of bad dreams. Dreams of Vivian and Lizzie, of being chased, cornered, caught, of vaulting on to the podium and being shoved off, of landing on her ankle – of searing pain, over and over again.

She was longing to go back to the Academy more than ever. If anyone had told her a week ago – when she was heading up to the National Sports Training Centre with such high hopes – that she'd be homesick for London, she would never have believed them. Now she could hardly wait to get back to Head-Over-Heels House, the park, the river and the Academy coaches – yes, even dear old Oleg, with his weird training plans and even stranger cures for injuries and ailments!

First there was the final training session to get through, and Barbara Steele would be watching. This was Ellie's chance to show someone other than Vivian what she was capable of. If Ellie wanted to get a call-back for the Euros selection weekend in six weeks' time, this was her chance. Vivian would never consider Ellie, but maybe if she could impress Barbara . . .

But there was a surprise in store for Ellie and the other Academy girls. They turned up in the gym and found Emma Bannerdown, Academy head coach, chatting with Barbara Steele and Vivian Ponting.

'Did you know Emma was coming?' asked Bella.

The others all shook their heads. Ellie couldn't help glancing over nervously at where Emma was deep in conversation with Vivian.

A couple of moments later, Emma came over to greet the Academy girls as they piled their kit into lockers.

'Morning, girls!' she said. 'Have you had a good week?'

Ellie thought Emma's eyes lingered a little longer on her as she asked this, so she nodded enthusiastically.

'I've been talking to Vivian about how you've each done,' Emma went on, glancing at Ellie again. 'She has some suggestions for the direction we need to take your training from here, with Euros selections in mind.'

'I bet she does,' whispered Katya.

'But she seems pleased with how most of you have performed on the camp.' Again Ellie felt that Emma looked at her as she said the words 'most of you'.

'Barbara Steele is taking the training session this morning,' Emma went on. 'I don't need to tell any of you how important it is for you to impress her. Ultimately, as head coach, she'll decide who gets a call-back for the selection weekend.'

Ellie felt her heart beating super fast. She felt suddenly like she had on the first day of camp, before Vivian had squashed all the confidence out of her: full of hope and ambition. She even forgot about her ankle for a couple of dizzying seconds.

'Think of today like a competition,' said Emma. 'Barbara's looking to see what new skills you've mastered on every piece of apparatus. You need to bring your A-game to every rotation.'

Buoyed up by Emma's speech, Ellie worked harder than she'd ever worked before in the warm-up. And in the stretching and conditioning she was pleased when Barbara complimented her on her line. Then it was back to apparatus work. Barbara walked around the rotations, asking questions and making notes in her jotter pad. Ellie was working on a Mo salto on the bars and Barbara was impressed.

'You fell on the bars at British Champs, am I right?' she asked when Ellie dismounted.

Ellie nodded, her face aflame. 'Um. Yes.'

'But you can do some very good skills in training

– better than anyone else in Junior squad,' Barbara added with a smile.

Ellie nodded. 'I suppose.'

'But can you bring them to competition?' Barbara was looking at her with her intense blue eyes.

'I think so,' said Ellie. 'That is – I've never messed up on bars before. It's my favourite piece.'

Barbara just nodded then said. 'Nice Mo, by the way. Hold the straddle shape a little longer and it'll be even tighter.'

On beam and floor Ellie felt she fared better. 'Ah – who could forget this routine!' she heard Barbara saying to Vivian and Emma as she went up to perform. 'Sensational choreography – Casey Cottrell, isn't it?'

Ellie couldn't help smiling. It was true that the former ballerina and ex-Olympic gymnast Casey Cottrell had devised Ellie's routine which combined hip-hop, ballet and sensational tumbling. Ellie had hated it at first. It had taken weeks of heartache before she'd come to love the electric routine which she now realised showed off her skills perfectly.

'She even gets a triple twist in that final tumble pass – rather than just the double,' said Emma. 'I tell you, some of our male gymnasts would be thrilled to be able to do that move.'

'*If* she can land it,' was all Vivian could say.

Ellie did land it. And even if it was agony on her swollen ankle, there was no way she was going to show that. She finished with a flourish and a smile big enough to rival one of Scarlett's.

But she still wasn't sure she'd done enough. Memory Danster was sensational on every single piece; Eva Reddle looked stronger than ever; and all the other gymnasts had made incredible progress during this one intense week of training. If Ellie wanted to be sure of a call-back to the selection weekend, she had to go all out.

The final rotation was the vault and by the time she got there Ellie was really struggling not to limp. But she was desperate to show Barbara how close she was to perfecting the Amanar, even though that meant going directly against Vivian's instructions.

The girls lined up at the start of the vault.

Memory was as untalkative as ever, her face creased into a frown as she stared at the vault. Ellie realised she'd never thanked her for not telling tales on her the other night. She wished suddenly that she had.

Scarlett was stretching and pouting and when she landed a perfect double, she smiled at Ellie sweetly and said, 'And that's how the big girls play!'

She didn't look quite so happy when Memory executed her Amanar perfectly and Katya said, 'That is how the big girls play, no?'

'Better to do a vault with a lower start value and execute it perfectly than go for a showy move and not even point your toes!' said Scarlett, cattily.

'Memory's execution was flawless,' Ellie said quickly.

The sullen-faced gymnast looked up quickly and shot her a look of – what? Surprise? Gratitude? But then she walked away without a word. Like Tam said, she was certainly hard to read.

But Scarlett wasn't done. As Ellie stood up to have her turn she said silkily, 'At least I'm not still stuck doing single twist like a kid at a regional gym comp!'

Ellie inhaled sharply. If she hadn't been sure what she was going to do before, she certainly was now. Her heart was pounding angrily as she waited for Barbara to give her the signal to start, then she took the run up at full speed. She tried to recall what had worked with Tam in the moonlit gym. Then she attempted to channel all the anger and hurt she been feeling recently to propel herself through the air. Her hands hit the vault with more aggression than she even knew she had inside her. She flew through the air, twisting once, twice – it was perfect. She'd rotated exactly right, and as she came into land she felt a brief moment of elation. She'd done it. She'd landed the Amanar in front of Vivian, Emma and Barbara Steele.

Then – a millisecond later – she felt the searing pain in her ankle.

Ellie cried out, and fell forwards, clutching her leg. The whole gym seemed to disappear for a long moment in a black wave of agony. Then it was spinning around her, people running to her, voices calling through the pain and, worse than anything, worse even than the acute searing agony in her foot, was the knowledge that she'd blown it. She'd thrown away her chance of making it to Euros. For good!

CHAPTER
Ten

'It's a stress fracture,' said the doctor, Sam. He showed her the X-ray on his tablet and pointed to a thin black line running through the heel bone. 'We often see them in high-level athletes who do a lot of running or jumping. Caused by high-impact landing on hard surfaces.'

Ellie's head was spinning and her foot was throbbing, but somehow she was still too shocked to cry.

'This kind of fracture can be hard to spot,' said Sam with a shake of his head that made his dreadlocks dance. 'Particularly if the patient isn't giving us the whole picture.' He looked at Ellie as he said this. She flushed but could not meet his eye. 'I suspect this has been causing you a lot of bother, right?'

Ellie looked down at her hands and said nothing.

'Did you really lie, Ellie?' asked Emma. She and Vivian had brought Ellie to Sam. In fact, Ellie was vaguely aware that it had been Vivian who had been the first to her side when she fell and that it had been the Australian coach who had carried her over to the surgery too.

Ellie felt the tears starting to come now. She nodded her head.

'And it's been hurting you a while?' said Vivian.

Ellie nodded her head again and sniffed to stop the drops that threatened to descend from her eyes.

'It's the kind of injury that can happen to any gymnast,' said Emma, reassuringly. 'It's unlucky.'

'But it's worse than it could have been because you hid it from us,' said Vivian. She sounded angry as she spoke, but when Ellie glanced up at her face she didn't look cross – more . . . upset.

'So, what can I do?' asked Ellie.

'I'm afraid that complete rest is the only option,' said Sam matter-of-factly.

'What?'

'I'm going to put you in a CAM boot to take all the pressure off and speed up healing,' he went on. 'All you need to do is put your feet up and you should be right as rain in six to ten weeks.'

'Ten weeks!' sobbed Ellie. 'But – that's . . . I can't. What about the selection weekend? What about Euros?'

She glanced desperately from Emma to Sam to Vivian, but they all wore the same serious expression.

'I'm sorry,' said Sam. 'I'm afraid there's nothing else for it.'

'But can't I keep up with *some* of the training?' asked Ellie. 'There must be stuff I can do even with the boot on?'

Again she glanced at Emma and Vivian. Emma looked uncertain, but Vivian said, 'I've got an idea. I'm going to make a few phone calls and we'll discuss it later, OK?'

*

78

Just a few hours later, Ellie stared out of the train window, her eyes red and puffy from crying. She'd shed so many tears since this morning she felt as if she must have dried up the salt well in her eyes. Now she was sitting on a train, heading home – and she didn't think she'd ever felt so miserable in her life. She had missed the creek like an ache in recent weeks, but now, as she watched the familiar Cornish coastline unravel before her, all she wanted was to be heading back to London with the other Academy gymnasts.

She kept running over the conversation she'd had with Emma before she left. 'Vivian believes this is the best thing for you. She has a friend in Cornwall. A coach she knows from Australia. She wants you to work with him.'

'A gym coach?'

'Not exactly.'

Ellie's head was spinning. 'I don't understand.'

'It will all make sense when you get home,' said Emma.

'But when can I come back to the Academy?'

Ellie heard herself saying. 'And what about Euros selections? Will I be able to go?'

'It all depends how quickly you heal,' said Emma.

'*And* how far I fall behind while I'm away from the Academy,' Ellie added unhappily.

'Don't think about it like that,' said Emma. 'Vivian is convinced this approach will benefit your gymnastics generally.'

'But she *hates* me,' Ellie wanted to say – although she didn't. Showing disrespect to a coach was a definite no-no in gymnastics. Ellie knew Emma would frown on it, and she also knew that once Emma's mind was made up there was no use trying to change it.

And so now here she was – not going back to the Academy on the minibus with all her friends, but on the train, heading towards Cornwall, filled with a feeling of sickening disappointment *and* agonising pain from her ankle. Every time she glanced down at her foot in its giant plastic boot she wanted to cry. The first time she'd tried walking in it she felt like one of the soldiers from the rehabilitation centre.

This must be how they felt, she thought.

Even her first sight of the ocean, glistening in the sun as the train skirted its way along the cliff tops, failed to lift her spirits as much as it usually did. The sea was the same deep blue as the practice floor, and the white wave tops reminded her of the foam blocks tumbling in the pit. It made her feel worse than ever.

The train drew into the station and Ellie lugged her heavy rucksack down on to the platform, almost falling flat on her face as she misjudged the distance stepping down in her big boot. But before she had the chance to feel really sorry for herself, she was mobbed by two excited figures.

'Ellie! It's so fab to see you! We missed you like crazy!'

Ellie was squished in a sandwich hug between her little sister and her best friend and for a second she thought she was going to cry again – only this time from happiness and relief.

'Ooh – look at that boot!' squeaked Lucy when she eventually released her.

'You look like a spaceman,' added Nancy with a grin.

Ellie looked from one to the other. They were both beaming and freckle-faced. Ellie realised how pale and sun-deprived she must look in comparison.

'I'm so sorry you're hurt,' said Lucy, hugging her arm tightly. 'But it's awesome to have you home!'

'And your timing is perfect!' said Nancy. 'The school holidays have just started so we'll totally be able to hang out all the time.'

Ellie just nodded. No matter how thrilled she was to see them, her heart was breaking at the same time. She was still half wishing she could turn around and go in the opposite direction.

Then she looked up to see Dad standing behind the girls, quiet and smiling in his old fisherman's jumper, his straw-coloured hair sticking up wildly from his head.

'Come here, my big girl!' he said, wrapping Ellie in his arms. He didn't need to say anything else. He just hugged her tight, and Ellie knew that he understood.

'We came in *Diablo*,' said Lucy excitedly. 'We thought you might like to travel in style back to the creek.'

'Sounds perfect!' Ellie managed to say, forcing a smile on to her face.

Lucy tucked her arm into Ellie's. 'We're so pleased you're back!'

'But we also want to get rid of you as soon as possible,' said Nancy, grabbing Ellie's other arm and taking her rucksack at the same time. 'You do too, right?'

Ellie nodded, relieved they understood. 'No offence to you lot, of course.'

'None taken,' said Nancy. 'Now come on, time and tide wait for no one – not even injured gymnasts!'

CHAPTER
Eleven

The journey on her father's boat, *Diablo*, lifted Ellie's spirits a little. Being out on the waves, the wind blowing her hair, the sun sparkling on the ocean. She could almost feel the colour creeping back to her cheeks and light returning ever so slightly to her tear-stained eyes.

They made their way out of the harbour and along the coast. It was holiday season, so all the little beaches were covered in brightly coloured tents and umbrellas, the coves littered with surfers and bodyboarders, kayakers exploring the caves and kids learning to sail.

Then, as they rounded the headland into the estuary, Ellie felt a sudden rush of joy. The creek looked almost more beautiful than she'd ever seen it. There were yachts and sailboats moored up in fleets for the summer months, the beach in front of the Ferryboat Inn was packed with kids making sandcastles and off the sailing club quay a flotilla of novice sailors scudded across the water, their sails fluttering like colourful butterflies.

Ellie took a deep breath and closed her eyes, letting the sounds and smells of the creek wash over her. She felt as if she'd been holding her breath for days, carrying round the secret of her injury for so long that her whole body had wrapped around it like a tight ball of anxiety. Now it was all out in the open, even though she was still worried, she felt like she could breathe again.

Finally they navigated their way into the quieter backwaters of the creek. Ellie couldn't help smiling as she caught sight of her father's boatyard, the pontoon and the little beach where she and Lucy had spent nearly every day of their childhood. And

85

beyond that Trengilly Cottage, with its whitewashed walls and blue shutters shining in the sunshine.

And there was Mum on the pontoon, waving like her arm would fall off. She'd dyed her hair again – this time a bright purple that looked a bit strange with the giant green woolly jumper and orange tie-dye trousers she was wearing with gold wellington boots – but Ellie thought she looked beautiful.

There was a tall man by Mum's side who Ellie didn't recognise. He wasn't waving. He had his hands in his pockets and was talking on his mobile phone, wearing a scowl on his face that reminded Ellie of Memory Danster.

'Who's that with Mum?' Ellie asked as the boat drew close enough to hear Mum's loud 'Hellooo!'s from the shore.

'That's Coach Langer,' said Nancy, her face lighting up. 'Wonder what he wants?'

'He's Nancy's new gig coach,' Lucy explained. 'She's crazy about him!'

'Not in that way!' said Nancy, pulling a face. 'He's just the most awesome coach ever. Seriously, he has four Olympic golds to prove it!'

Coach Langer looked about thirty but his skin was so tanned and leathery it looked like crocodile hide. He'd probably been good looking once upon a time, but now he just looked cross.

'He doesn't usually do house calls,' Nancy was saying. 'I wonder what he wants?'

But there was no time to discuss it because before Dad had even moored up *Diablo*, Ellie was scrambling out on to the pontoon – risking a dunking – to be enfolded in a giant bear hug from her mum. She stunk of oil paint and white spirit – smells of her painting studio that made Ellie feel at home.

'Oh, my poor darling!' Mum was saying, looking at Ellie's space boot and taking in her pale face and red-rimmed eyes in dismay. Ellie hated the anxious way everyone seemed to be looking at her – it made her feel even more like a broken invalid than ever.

'Now, I've made you some special get-well recipes,' Mum was saying.

Ellie exchanged a look with Nancy and Lucy.

87

Mum was famous for her wacky food combos – some of which worked and some which very much didn't!

'And I found you an old pair of crutches, although I can't for the devil of me remember where I put them!' She scratched her head absent-mindedly, as if she might have tucked the crutches into her ponytail the way she often did with paintbrushes.

Ellie laughed. 'I don't need crutches, Mum.'

'The boot is to protect her foot and immobilise the fracture,' Lucy explained. 'But Ellie can walk on it.'

'In fact, she needs to,' Nancy added. 'So she maintains as much mobility as possible while she's healing. Otherwise she'll go back to gymnastics with loss of muscle tone and flexibility.'

'And that can take as long to get back from as the fracture itself,' added Lucy, who had been Googling Ellie's injury.

'Right,' said Mum, shaking her head, and Ellie could tell that she hadn't understood at all. 'That reminds me – Mr Langer here has come to chat with you, Ellie. About all of that sort of stuff.'

Ellie turned to Langer in surprise. He was just finishing up on the phone but he looked at her slightly impatiently, as if she'd somehow kept *him* waiting.

'Me?' she said. 'I thought – I mean, aren't you Nancy's coach?'

'Sure am,' said Langer with a lazy Australian drawl that sounded horribly like Vivian's. 'But now I'm yours too.'

'Mine? I . . .' Ellie stammered. 'I don't understand.'

'She's a wily one that Vivian – could talk Eskimos into buying ice-cubes.' He smiled wryly. 'Anyway, she's persuaded me to take you on to the team.'

'On our team!' Nancy shrieked excitedly. 'That is awesome, but how . . .?'

'But I don't . . .' Ellie started to say. 'I mean. There must be a mistake. I'm not a rower. I'm a gymnast.'

'Yup – I know!' said Langer, as if he was even less happy about the idea than Ellie was. 'But you know Vivvy.'

89

Ellie felt more and more like she didn't know Vivian Ponting at all.

'This is epic! Is Ellie really joining the gig team?' said Nancy.

'Looks like it!' said Langer drily. 'And as it happens we're a man down so you can sub in for the time being.'

'A man down?' said Nancy, her face falling. 'Who?'

'Why don't we go inside and discuss it over one of your mum's incredible cakes?' said Langer. Ellie noticed that the word 'incredible' was pronounced with a roll of his eyes which made her think he was familiar with Mum's unique style of baking.

But she was too confused to feel hungry. 'It just doesn't make any sense,' she murmured.

'It will,' said Langer. 'It will!'

CHAPTER
Twelve

Ellie's mum served up strawberry and spinach flapjacks, which were actually seriously nice, and crab and almond tarts, which really weren't. But they all pretended to like them anyway!

'I read somewhere that almonds are good for healing broken bones,' said Mum. 'And shellfish too, so I thought . . .'

'They're delicious, Mum,' said Ellie, cramming the last of her tart in her mouth and trying to swallow it quickly, before the bizarre combination hit her taste buds.

They were all sitting around the kitchen table.

Langer had propped his long legs up on the Aga whilst Nancy perched on the windowsill, looking more excited than Ellie had ever seen her. Lucy kept bobbing up and down, unable to sit still for longer than a minute.

Langer had been explaining everything. He might speak in the same long slow Aussie drawl as Vivian, but that was where the resemblance between the two coaches ended. Langer was a man of giant proportions, with black hair and chocolate brown eyes that sort of reminded Ellie of Tam's. And it was easy to see how he'd been a medal-winning rower – his legs were like tree trunks and his arm muscles bulged like some kind of superhero's.

'So how do you know Vivian?' Nancy was asking. 'I mean – talk about a small world!'

'Not so small really,' said Langer. 'We met when we were both competing at the Olympics. I was rowing for Aus and she was doing all that gym nonsense.'

Ellie flinched. She couldn't believe she was going to be coached by someone who didn't even like gymnastics.

'And you stayed in touch?' asked Nancy.

'Off and on,' Langer said, helping himself to another flapjack. 'Still, I was a bit surprised when she rang me up yesterday.'

'And what did you say?'

'At first I said that one ex-gymnast on my team was quite enough to deal with!' Langer rolled his eyes.

'Hey!' said Nancy. Langer grinned back at her but all Ellie could think of was the word 'ex'. Did Vivian think she was already out of the game?

'I only agreed to help because Matthew Jones broke his collarbone playing rugby at the weekend and that means I'm missing my five,' said Langer. Nancy groaned.

'I don't want to be rude,' said Ellie, carefully. 'But I need to be ready for Euros selections in six weeks. I need to spend every spare minute in the gym.'

'Don't see you doing too much of that with your space boot on, d'you?' said Langer.

'There's lots of stuff I can still practise whilst I'm getting better,' Ellie said quickly.

'Then why'd Vivvy send you here, eh?' said Langer.

'If she thought you should be doing cartwheels in your boot, I guess she wouldn't have banished you to deepest, darkest Cornwall, would she?'

Ellie stiffened. She knew he was right. She could have had her recovery at the Academy, kept up her core fitness, worked on non-impact skills. But Vivian had insisted on sending her away. For what? So she could join a rowing team?

'Nah, little Vivvy has a plan for you,' said Langer. 'She wants you up and on the water at six a.m. sharp tomorrow morning and every day – including weekends.'

Ellie could barely believe what she was hearing. Every time she thought things were as bad as they could get, they seemed to get worse.

'And she wants a weekly report on your progress,' Langer added. 'So if this Euros selections thing means anything to you, slacking is not an option.'

CHAPTER
Thirteen

That night, Lucy, Nancy and Ellie were all squeezed together in the little bedroom in the eaves that Ellie had shared with her sister but which was now Nancy and Lucy's. Nancy had insisted on giving Ellie her old bed back and was now camped out on an ancient blow-up mattress.

'We can't have old Bigfoot on the floor,' she insisted. She was wearing a pair of men's pyjamas with a funny nightcap which made her look like something out of a nursery rhyme. 'Especially now you're my teammate. I need you match fit ASAP!'

Ellie sighed. She still hadn't got her head round

the idea of being on the gig team but Nancy was over the moon, and even Mum and Dad were supportive.

'It'll be good for you to widen your interests, darling!' Mum had said at supper time. 'You're so focused on gym.'

'But Mum, you're like that with painting,' said Ellie. 'When you're into a picture you forget the rest of the world exists.'

'Sometimes you forget *we* exist, Mum,' agreed Lucy. 'I brought you a cup of tea in your studio the other day and you didn't know my name.'

'Darling, that was different,' said Mum. 'Art is my career.'

'And gym is mine!' said Ellie. 'And a gymnast's career can be over by the time she's twenty. Which means I need to focus on this now. I can have other interests later.'

'I suppose you're right,' Mum sighed. 'I just never expected to hear my fourteen-year-old daughter talking about her career.'

'Dad knows that's how it is,' said Ellie, turning to him in appeal. 'It was the same with Lizzie.'

'Lizzie worked hard and she played hard,' Dad said with a gentle smile. 'I think that's what made her seem so alive as a gymnast.'

Ellie recalled the footage she'd seen of Lizzie performing – the joy, the vitality she brought to the sport.

'I think that's what stopped her falling apart when it all came to an end.' Dad continued looking at Ellie meaningfully. 'She made gymnastics her life but – at the time – she could see there was life beyond gymnastics too.'

He turned and smiled at Ellie's mum, who for some reason was grinning back like a Cheshire cat. 'All I'm saying, Ellie,' he carried on, 'is that if this coach of yours thinks a bit of gig rowing will help your gym as well as widening your horizons, then what's not to like – eh?'

'I suppose,' said Ellie. She knew there was no point arguing. Vivian had made this part of her recovery programme. And if the Junior GB squad coach told her to take up rowing, she had no choice.

'Anyway, you need a bit of sun on your face,

Ellie,' said Nancy, as they all clambered into bed later. 'You look so pale I've been worrying you might have become a secret vampire!'

'Best watch out in the night then,' laughed Ellie, putting the lamp under her chin and pulling a funny face. 'Or I might take a nibble on your neck!'

Ellie lay in bed for ages after that, listening to the soft lapping of the waves on the shore, the rhythmic splash that had rocked her to sleep throughout her childhood and which she had missed so desperately when she first went to London. After a few minutes she could hear the soft purring of Nancy's snores and her sister's low sleeping breaths. In the gloom she could make out their sleeping figures, one curled up tightly in a ball, the other sprawled out over the bed like a starfish and she smiled, grateful they were here. She wasn't sure she could face the next few weeks alone. Dad had talked about life beyond gymnastics, but gym had been her life for so long that she was terrified to think of a future without it. Even a few weeks out of the gym seemed unbearable.

But she had no choice but to try.

CHAPTER
Fourteen

'Right, team, let's get this boat on the road.'

It was not even six a.m. The sun was barely awake and Ellie was standing shivering on the sailing club pontoon alongside Nancy and the four other members of the Creek Under-16s gig team, being yelled at by a giant of a man wearing a Hawaiian shirt and surf shorts.

'If you think I enjoy coaching a load of Pommy kids in this freezing cold weather you Brits call summer, then you've got another think coming!' he yelled.

'So why is he over here then?' asked Ellie, as they

dragged the gig boat into the water. 'Why doesn't he just go back to Bondi Beach or wherever?'

'He gets bored easily,' Nancy explained. 'At least that's what he says. Always looking for a new challenge. We are his latest project.'

'Lucky us!' said Ellie, rolling her eyes. Trying to lift a boat with a boot on wasn't exactly easy, but Langer was making no allowances for her.

'So, Boot Girl,' said Langer. 'Whatcha got in those arms of yours, eh? You as strong as our gym-girl Nancy, I wonder?'

Ellie shrugged. As the pontoon rocked under her feet, she was aware of how unstable the boot made her feel. The sense of wobbliness was unfamiliar – and disconcerting.

'She's probably got way more muscles than these wimps here.' Nancy tipped her head towards the boys who made up the other members of the crew. Ellie had actually known most of them her whole life – that's just how it was growing up on the creek – and it was funny to see Nancy rowing with Joe and Charlie, the two boys she'd beaten in the regatta the first time she'd visited Cornwall. There was also Nye Patterson, a tall, uber-cool kid from Port Navas and a copper-headed pocket dynamo called Peter Smith from Calamansack. Along with herself and Nancy they made up the Creek Under-16s gig team.

'Yeah, well just remember we don't need any silly somersaulting in this boat,' said Charlie, smirking at Nancy.

'Gigging is about strength – pure and simple,' added his mate Joe. 'And if you don't cut it you let the whole team down.'

Ellie nodded. She knew how much this meant to Nancy and so she was determined to give it her best, if only for her friend.

'You'll need to be a quick learner too,' Langer went on. 'We've got no time to carry dead wood in the boat if we're gonna be ready for the racing season.'

'Racing?' said Ellie. 'I – I mean . . . I'm not planning on staying in Cornwall for that long.'

'Way I hear it, you're here until you pass fit and get the call-back,' said Langer.

'Yes, but . . .'

'But nothing,' said Langer. 'Till then you're in my team and that means you get ready for race season like everyone else.'

There was nothing she could say. Ellie knew Langer was right. And she also knew she might never get that call-back. With every day she spent in Cornwall, her Euros dream slipped further and further away.

'He's tougher than Oleg,' she whispered to Nancy as they got ready to get in the boat.

'I know,' grinned Nancy. 'Brilliant, isn't he!'

'Does he actually have a first name?' Ellie asked.

'Terry,' said Nancy. 'But nobody ever calls him that. You call him Coach Langer if he's in a good mood . . .'

'And if he's in a bad one . . .?'

'Sir or Your Majesty,' said Nancy. 'That's if he hasn't snapped your head off for daring to speak at all.'

'He sounds just like Vivian!' grimaced Ellie. 'Do you think they feed Aussie coaches some kind of mean pill or something?'

'Oh, he's only being cruel to be kind,' said Nancy, who had tugged on her life jacket and was clambering into the boat. 'Pain is power – that's his mantra.'

'Sounds familiar!' said Ellie. 'Well, I can do the pain bit. I guess we'll see about the rest.'

It wasn't easy getting into the gig boat with her boot on. Nancy gave Ellie a hand, but she still wobbled like mad before taking her seat in the middle of the boat. The sun was just starting to cast a golden glow over the water, and all the boats on the pontoon were bobbing in the choppy waves, making a concert of sloshing noises that mingled with the cries of the seagulls in the morning air. Ellie sighed. She couldn't feel totally miserable when she was surrounded by all this. But still . . .

'We'll just be training on the creek for the moment,' Langer was saying. 'Then when the new kid's up to it we'll try the open water.'

Nancy was rowing stroke, which meant she was at the back of the boat, in the stern, setting the pace for the others. Ellie was just in front of her as five, rowing on the right, bow side. Langer was cox, which meant he sat in the stern seat facing Nancy and the rest of the crew, yelling stuff like, 'Hold water . . . Easy oars . . . ship your kit.'

'It's like a foreign language!' giggled Ellie.

'No weirder than gymnastics, though, is it?' said Nancy. 'Sheep jumps . . . tick-tocks . . . back tucks and all that nonsense.'

'The beginning of the stroke is called the catch,' Langer was saying, glaring at the two girls. 'It's tempting to use your arms, but a great rower gets their legs behind the stroke right from the catch. OK?'

Ellie pushed her boot against the stretcher and felt a familiar twinge.

'What do you think you're doing, Boot Girl?' Langer yelled. 'Are you totally off your head? You push off like that from your crock foot, you'll do damage with every stroke. You might as well jump up and down on it.'

Ellie flushed. It was just like being yelled at by Vivian, but in a boatful of sniggering boys it was even more humiliating. 'Then how?'

'Vivvy wants you using your good leg only.'

'Seriously,' said Joe, who was sitting behind her. 'She's rowing with only *one* leg?'

'Yes, she is!' Langer snapped. 'You got a problem with that, Bruton?'

'Um, no,' said Joe quickly.

'Any fool knows it's your arms and your back that link the leg drive to the handle of the oar and do all the work,' said Langer. 'Got it, Boot Girl?'

'Um, I think so.'

'You're gonna need strong core muscles for this job,' Langer went on. 'It'll work up those namby-pamby arms of yours too. You reckon you're up to it?'

'Just watch while this namby-pamby gymnast puts all these boys to shame,' said Nancy, pulling a face.

Ellie smiled at her gratefully. She'd missed training with Nancy so much. Missed the way Nancy could make a joke out of even the grimmest workout, make everything seem fun with a single grin or a quip. And being part of a team was a new challenge. As a gymnast she'd always competed individually, even at team events, and now it felt quite different knowing she had to match her movements to the pace set by Nancy, that she had to be in perfect sync with the other crew members, all pulling together to slice the boat over the water.

It wasn't easy. Ellie might be in great shape from the Academy and National squad camp, but this required a different kind of fitness. It didn't help that she was only allowed to push off from one leg, leaving the other sitting in the bottom of the boot, large, heavy and useless. And no matter how she tried, she couldn't quite keep up with the rhythm. Langer continued to yell, 'Up one. One up . . . hold water, hit the catch! TIMING, Ellie!' as Ellie puffed and sweated and heaved. She was used to intense, gruelling training sessions at the Academy, but this was brutal in a totally different way.

And then, just when she thought she was starting to get it, Ellie caught a crab. 'It's what you say when a rower loses control,' Nancy had explained to her over breakfast. 'Sometimes if the pace is too much for you, your oar gets stuck in the water or you break a pin – or both, and that's called catching a crab!'

'And then what happens?' Ellie had asked.

'Oh, your whole oar can snap in half,' said Nancy cheerfully. 'Or you get toppled out of the boat – or both. But don't panic – the rest of the boat will keep rowing. You just have to get your oar back between the pins and rejoin the stroke when you're able.'

But when it actually happened out on the water, Ellie forgot Nancy's warning and completely panicked. She failed to lift her oar on time and lost control, accidentally pushing against the board with her bad foot, and feeling a red hot shot of pain through her ankle. For a second she thought her oar was going to break in half as the other blades swooped and sliced around her.

'Just get back into the stroke,' yelled Langer. 'What are you waiting for?'

Ellie's ankle screamed in pain and she could barely catch her breath or remember what to do.

'Get back in the stroke!' Langer yelled again.

Determined not to be beaten, Ellie took a deep breath and tried to ignore the agony in her foot. Timing was everything. If she got it wrong she'd catch another crab immediately. It was like a complex vault or a manoeuvre on the bar: getting the exact angle and the exact timing was the difference between a clean landing and total wipeout. She watched the oars slicing rhythmically through the water, lifting, twisting. She waited for the perfect moment, then plunged her oar back into the water. To her relief, this time it didn't stick.

'Good work!' yelled Langer. It was the first compliment he'd paid Ellie all morning and she was surprised at how happy it made her feel.

She managed to avoid losing the oar again and by the end of the session she was starting to get into something like a steady rhythm.

'You were awesome!' said Nancy as they clambered off at the sailing club pontoon. 'Which of course I knew you would be!'

'Not bad for a first-timer,' said Joe with a grin.

'Yeah – you're all right,' said Charlie. 'For a girl.'

'Admit it – she was epic!' said Nancy.

'You done OK,' was all Langer could say. 'But I see what Vivvy meant about building you up a bit.'

Ellie flushed. She wanted to remind him she was only there because of a power-crazed gym coach who had decided to make her life a misery because of her surname. But he was a friend of Vivian's and she knew it would only get back to her.

'See you all tomorrow,' Langer said. 'And maybe the new kid can go at something more than a snail's pace.'

Ellie turned to Nancy as Langer strolled away. 'That was you guys going slow?'

'Oh, yeah. That was just a little dawdle, really,' said Nancy with a shrug. 'And in easy conditions too. Just wait till we get you out to sea. That's where the fun really starts.'

'You have a strange idea of fun!' laughed Ellie.

'Come on,' said Nancy as they made their way back to Trengilly Cottage. 'I know exactly what you need.'

'A new ankle,' Ellie suggested.

'Can't manage that, I'm afraid,' said Nancy. 'But I reckon we scoff down some of your mum's bacon and berry scones and then there's only one thing for it – you need an emergency gym fix!'

Nancy was right. Ellie was longing to do gymnastics so much her body felt almost twitchy, even though she was in so much pain!

'You know me so well!' she smiled.

'You can still do conditioning and stuff,' said Nancy. 'Vivian hasn't said you can't do that.'

'Not yet!' said Ellie, rolling her eyes.

'So let's get out of this damp gear and get you back in the splits, you crazy gym-addict!'

CHAPTER
Fifteen

Less than an hour later, Ellie found herself standing in front of the building where she had first learned to do a forward roll when she was just four years old. Dad always told her she'd been flinging herself over pieces of furniture and turning herself upside down on the beach as soon as she could walk, until he'd finally given in and accepted that the gym was the only place for her. Ellie had loved it from the very moment she stepped through the doors.

She had so many happy memories of this place. Training, competitions, friendships. Every single piece of equipment was suffused with memories;

even the battered changing room and tired-looking waiting area made her feel happier than she had in weeks. It felt like coming home.

Her old coach Fran was delighted to see her. She was working with a group of younger girls but as soon as they'd finished she came over and gave Ellie a big hug.

'It's great to see you, Ellie! You look -' Fran hesitated. Ellie knew that she could read her face like a book. 'You look tired.'

'Oh, we had to get up early,' Ellie explained. 'Vivian's insisting I do gig rowing with Nancy.'

'Hmm,' said Fran. 'I'm not sure that's the sort of tired I mean . . . but, yes, I've heard all about Vivian's unorthodox fitness regime.'

'She told you?'

'She did,' said Fran. 'We've also been chatting about what you should be doing – and *not* doing – in here.'

'Did you tell her you think the rowing is completely wrong for me?' asked Ellie hopefully.

Fran smiled. 'No – because I don't.'

Ellie's face fell. She'd been hoping Fran would be on her side.

'Listen. I've known Vivian for years. We competed against each other, and no one could beat Vivian Ponting except your aunt. What I remember most about her – apart from the crazy way she carried on at competitions – was her incredible all-around fitness. While the rest of us were in the gym she was out surfing or paddle-boarding or cliff jumping. We all thought she was mad when we first met her but we came to respect her sheer power.'

'That may have worked for her, but that doesn't mean it's right for Ellie,' said Lucy, who was wearing her Cornish squad leo with pride.

'Maybe,' said Fran. 'Who knows. But Ellie can't keep up a full training programme in the gym until her foot is healed, so where's the harm in giving it a go in the meantime?'

'I suppose there's not,' Ellie conceded reluctantly. 'I just feel – like Vivian's written me off.'

'Wait till you see the detailed training programme she's devised for you,' said Fran. 'If she thought you were a no-hoper I doubt she'd have made such a lot of effort to think about how to keep you in peak condition. Here, I'll show you.'

Fran went into the office and emerged a few moments later with a file. It was filled with incredibly detailed instructions for Ellie's training. It had been designed to work on her strengths whilst keeping all pressure off her foot. Although Ellie still didn't understand why she couldn't do this programme with Bella and Kashvi and Katya and all the others back at the Academy, perhaps the Junior National squad coach hadn't written her off completely.

She tried to push her worries aside and throw herself into training. It felt so good to be back here, especially with Lucy. Her little sister had made a ton of progress over the last year and Ellie felt so proud watching her. But although Lucy was incredibly talented on floor, her bar and vault were less confident. 'I don't have the strength,' she admitted to Ellie.

'Well, Vivian's programme for Ellie puts a lot of emphasis on strength and conditioning,' said Fran. 'You should join in too!'

So the two sisters worked side by side through Vivian's gruelling workout. Ellie enjoyed it far more than she expected.

But as well as the conditioning and the endless one leg balances and spins, Vivian had her working on weirder stuff too. With her boot off, she had to roll a tennis ball beneath her injured foot, rotating it through a figure of eight. Ellie couldn't for the life of her see how it was helping her gymnastics.

'Vivvy knows what she's doing,' said Fran. 'Sometimes you just have to trust that the coach has your best interests at heart.'

'But what if they don't?' said Ellie, stopping her figures of eight and looking up anxiously.

Fran raised an eyebrow. Ellie knew she was close to stepping over the line. 'There is no reason on earth why Vivian would do anything other than what she thinks is best for your gymnastics.'

'I can think of one or two reasons!' muttered Nancy when Fran had walked away.

'More like seven,' added Lucy.

'Um – why seven?' asked Ellie.

'Cos that's how many times Lizzie won the gold and Vivian had to settle for silver!'

That evening they Skyped Tam and Katya, who were home from squad camp and settled back in to Head-Over-Heels House in London. They hadn't spoken to Ellie since their hasty and tearful farewells at the National Sports Training Centre the day before, so they were dying to know all her news. Katya looked horrified when she heard about Ellie's new training regime.

'If Vivian made me go on a boat to train, I would be giving up gymnastics for good!' Katya announced.

Lucy laughed. They all remembered how Katya had refused to set foot in a boat ever again after her snowy sea adventure last Christmas.

'It's a bit unusual,' admitted Tam. 'But I guess it'll build up your core fitness.'

'If it doesn't kill me first,' said Ellie. 'I've never ached so much after a gym training session.'

It was true. Her first gigging session had made

her hurt in muscles she hadn't even known she had.

'I always said gym was for wimps,' laughed Nancy.

'Well, we Academy wimps are all missing Ellie,' said Tam. 'It felt all wrong coming back to London without her. Everyone sends their love.'

'And they is wishing you speedy getting-well,' added Katya.

'Oleg wants to send you some special home-made Romanian ointment to help mend your foot quicker,' grinned Tam. 'Apparently it's made of the sweat glands of a Eurasian lynx, mixed with herbs from his mother's garden. I'm not sure I'd go near the stuff myself!'

'It smells very bad,' said Katya, wrinkling up her nose. 'I think it will make your foot fall off, not get better.'

'Still, it's nice of him to think of me,' said Ellie.

'Everyone is thinking of you,' said Tam. 'Well, maybe except Scarlett. She's just pleased to have a rival out of the way.'

'She's probably plotting ways to take out the rest of the GB squad as we speak,' added Nancy with a grin.

'I guess I'm totally out of the running for Euros now, aren't I?' sighed Ellie, feeling her heart ache with the unfairness of it all.

'Not necessarily,' said Katya. 'Selection camp is still six weeks away. Maybe you will be recovered by then.'

'How's the ankle doing?' asked Tam, frowning. Ellie knew Tam blamed himself for her injury – for encouraging her to go for the Amanar, for not spotting that she was hurt. In the chaos of goodbyes the previous day, he'd been more upset than anyone. Ellie had tried to tell him none of this was his fault – that she was the one who'd been stupid, careless. But she could see from the expression in his eyes that he still felt awful. 'Oh, fine,' Ellie lied, forcing a smile on to her face to try and reassure him. 'I feel better already.'

The truth was that the pain was still intense. Doctor Sam had said it might start to hurt more as it began to heal and Ellie desperately hoped he was right, but she was terrified that it was getting worse rather than better.

CHAPTER

Sixteen

The days at home flew by – first a week, then a fortnight. National squad camp seemed like a distant memory and the Academy, where the other gymnasts were training hard without her, felt like it was a million miles away. Ellie found herself fitting all-too-easily back into the rhythm of Cornish life. Gig training times were dependent on the tides, but nothing, not even torrential rain, kept them off the water. Then there was gym, working on Vivian's programme. Ellie might not always be happy with her training methods, but at least Vivian didn't seem to have forgotten about her. She checked regularly on Ellie's progress and modified her training schedule accordingly.

In between sporting activities, the girls made the most of the fact Ellie was home and that there was no school. They spent lazy times on the beach, out on the creek or visiting the little local coves dotted around the coastline.

Two weeks after her arrival in Cornwall, Langer decided that Ellie was finally ready for ocean gigging. He and the other crew members arranged to meet the girls at one of the town's busy tourist beaches, so after gym, Lucy, Ellie and Nancy changed out of their leotards into shorts and T-shirts and made their way down the hill to the sandy cove. They were early, so they sat and picnicked in the sunshine, watching children jumping in the waves and clambering over the rocks armed with buckets and nets.

'We used to come rock pooling here when we were younger,' Ellie told Nancy as they tucked into Mum's special recipe Cornish pasties. Their dad had warned them not to ask about the 'special' ingredient that morning. 'You're probably best off not knowing!' he'd said.

'Can we get buckets and nets and try it sometime?' asked Nancy. 'I'd like to catch a crab – a real one, not a gigging one, that is!'

'Ooh, yes,' said Lucy, who had been staring curiously at the contents of her pasty. 'There are great pools at low tide. There's even an old shipwreck just by the headland.'

'A proper one?' asked Nancy.

'Yup, a big ship ran aground in a storm there about fifty years ago,' said Ellie. 'It's on the seabed, just where those kayakers are now.' She pointed out to the headland and Nancy squinted in the direction of her finger.

'At low tide you can walk out there and see it,' said Lucy. 'It's a bit spooky but kind of cool.'

'Does the tide really go out that far?' asked Nancy.

'Yeah, it shelves pretty sharply – at low tide this whole coastline is totally different,' Ellie explained.

'There are caves and gullies that turn into beaches for a few hours, then disappear,' added Lucy.

'Which makes it dangerous if you're not familiar with the tides,' said Ellie. 'Tourists are always getting cut off and needing to be rescued.'

'I like the idea of a shipwreck,' said Nancy, laying back and patting her pasty-filled belly contentedly. 'I think it'd be a pretty cool way to go.'

'Ooh – no!' said Lucy. 'You could be eaten by a shark – or munched by fishes!'

'I suppose you two would rather be squashed to death by a falling beam or suffocated under a pile of foam blocks in the pit,' laughed Nancy.

'Well, I think we all need to stick around for a little while longer,' said Ellie. 'It's race season coming up – as Langer *keeps* reminding us!'

Half an hour later Langer and the rest of the crew met them at the beach and they set off from the shelter of the cove out to the vast expanse of the ocean. The sea wasn't that choppy – just a small squally wind creating little scuds across the water. In *Diablo*, it would have felt calm as a millpond, but in the light gig the little waves felt more like mountains. Ellie could see why Langer had made her practice so much in the estuary.

These days she was confident in her rhythm and able to keep pace with the others, even with her one-footed rowing style. She hadn't caught a crab in ages. But although she'd made progress in the sheltered waters of the creek, nothing prepared her for the open ocean. The swell of the waves seemed to run completely counter to the rhythm she'd worked so hard to master, and no matter how much attack the team put into every stroke, they always seemed to be fighting a force determinedly set against them.

All the same, there was something incredibly exciting about it, and Ellie managed to put aside the pain in her ankle and her thoughts of the unfathomable depths beneath, and enjoy the sensation of fighting against the elements with just a thin piece of wood in her hands.

'You're getting the hang of it,' Langer said after the first sea session was over. 'We'll make a gigger of you yet, Boot Girl.'

'I don't want to be a gigger,' Ellie reminded him, although she couldn't help flushing happily. 'I want to be a gymnast.'

'I believe the second bit,' Langer said with a slow smile. 'But I'm not so sure about the first. You almost looked like you were enjoying it out there today. I swear I saw a hint of a smile on the Boot Girl's face.'

'That wasn't a smile,' said Nancy, appearing from behind. 'It was a grimace. Even Oleg's ice baths don't make Ellie pull faces as bad as that, you know.'

'I *am* enjoying it more than I thought I would, actually,' Ellie admitted. 'Still, I can't wait till I'm all better and I can get back to the gym properly.'

'Well, don't go hurrying off too soon,' said Langer. 'We need you for race season – no sign of Matthew Jones being back at the oar just yet.'

'When does race season start?' Ellie asked Nancy as they made their way back across the beach to where Dad and Lucy were waiting for them in the Land Rover.

'Last weekend of August,' said Nancy. 'I hate to say it, but I kind of hope you're gone by then.'

'That's the date of the selection weekend – up at the National Sports Training Centre,' said Ellie, her heart doing a somersault. For a few minutes, out there on the water, she'd forgotten all about Euros, but now her old hopes and fears came washing over her again in a giant wave.

'Any word from Vivian on whether you'll be invited to go?' asked Nancy.

'Nope,' said Ellie. 'But Emma's coming down to see me the week after next. She's judging Grades down here, I think, so she's popping into the gym. And I have a hospital appointment just before, so I guess I'll know how my ankle's healing by then too.'

'Does it feel any better?' asked Nancy, looking down curiously at Ellie's boot, as if it were a science experiment.

Ellie nodded, and this time she meant it. She really did feel like her ankle might be getting better. It had been hurting less and less lately – even doing Vivian's funny exercise with the ball was getting easier.

'I think so,' she said. 'But it's hard to tell. Since I started gigging, every bit of my body hurts all the time – perhaps I just don't notice it any more!'

CHAPTER
Seventeen

'So are you excited about your Grades?' Katya asked Lucy over Skype the following week. The two girls had recently declared themselves 'Skype sisters' because they spent so much time chatting every night. 'Have you got butterflies in your tummy?'

'All the time!' said Lucy. 'I'm so scared I'm sure I'm going to faint on the beam or throw up on the floor and blow the whole thing.'

'Of course you won't,' said Tam who was perched next to Katya at the giant dining table in Head-Over-Heels House. He was peering into the screen with a bacon buttie in one hand and a chocolate brownie in the other, taking bites from them alternately. Ellie still found it weird to talk to him and Katya, knowing they were in London, working hard at the Academy, sitting down to supper every night with all the Head-Over-Heelers and getting ready for the big selection weekend. It was everything she longed to be doing herself. 'You'll ace it, win a medal . . .'

'And a place at the Academy too!' added Nancy. 'At least that's what a little bird called Fran told me!'

'No, that's too much,' said Lucy, but her cheeks blushed pink with pleasure.

'You're turning into a brilliant gymnast,' said Nancy. 'I may not compete myself any more, but I know talent when I see it.'

'It *would* be a dream come true to be an Academy girl!' sighed Lucy.

'And a dream for me too!' said Katya. 'To have my favourite Cornish BFF in Head-Over-Heels House with me!'

'Talking of the Academy, how is everyone?' asked Nancy. 'Come on, bro, what's the latest gossip?'

'Oh, I should have told you!' said Tam. 'Kashvi has quit!'

'What?' said all three Cornish girls together.

'You're not serious,' said Ellie.

'Deadly serious,' said Tam.

'But – I mean – she's an incredible gymnast,' said Ellie. 'Why would she give it all up?'

'Oh but she has not given it *all* up,' Katya added. 'She is just moving to rhythmic.'

Ellie was speechless for a moment. Rhythmic gymnastics was so different to the artistic discipline. There were no bars, no beams, no vault – just floor work, with a greater dance element and less acrobatics – and more props: balls, ribbons, hoops and so on. Ellie was forced to admit to herself that it was everything that Kashvi was so good at. But why had she made the change now?

'Vivian came to the gym to see all the GB squad girls,' said Tam, as if he had heard her question. Then he added gently, 'She invited them all to the selection weekend.'

Ellie felt her stomach turn and thought she might

be sick. 'That's great,' she said, her voice sounding far-off and distant. 'Seriously – amazing.'

'All except Kashvi,' Katya went on. 'She wasn't invited.'

'Why?' asked Ellie, still fighting back the urge to cry. She could feel Tam looking at her anxiously so she did her best to keep her face straight.

'Vivian told Kashvi she'd never make it with artistic but she stood a chance with rhythmic,' said Tam.

'She got her a try out for the rhythmic GB squad,' added Katya. 'And that was that. She's leaving the Academy.'

'Just like that?' asked Nancy in astonishment.

'She has to – we don't do rhythmic.'

'She is moving to Bath,' said Katya, who had tugged one leg behind her head and was sitting quite comfortably in that position. 'I was confused about this at first – until Tam tell me Bath is a town too!'

'The GB rhythmic squad is based at Bath University,' said Tam with a grin. 'Kashvi's already made a big splash, apparently. They reckon she might be in with a chance for the next Olympic squad.'

'That's great,' said Ellie, still feeling numb. 'But . . .' She couldn't put all she wanted to say in words. How much she'd miss Kashvi – her sense of fun, her loyalty, her kindness as a friend – and how devastated Ellie would feel herself if she had to leave behind three of the pieces of apparatus she'd trained on for so long. Most of all, how sad it felt to know that more of her friends were falling by the wayside.

She couldn't help remembering her first day at the Academy – it felt like so long ago now – when Emma had said that not many of them would make it to the top flight of gymnastics. She hadn't wanted to believe it, but now Nancy had given up gym completely, Camille had an injury and might never get back in a leotard again, Kashvi was moving to a different discipline, and Ellie had no idea if her ankle would heal and allow her to compete once more. It felt like their original little squad was falling apart.

'I guess Scarlett is thrilled,' said Nancy, pulling what Lucy called her 'Scarlett face'. 'One less rival for a spot on the Euros squad.'

'Actually, I think it's rattled her,' said Tam. 'Vivian's weeding out the gymnasts she doesn't think will cut it. I think Scarlett's worried she may be next.'

Ellie's heart contracted again. Had Vivian already weeded her out? She'd invited the others to the selection weekend, but not Ellie. Had she finally made up her mind that Ellie wasn't worth bothering with?

Ellie shoved the thought to one side. She refused to let herself think that it was all over. After all, Emma was coming next week, and if Ellie could show her how well she was progressing, then perhaps she'd tell Vivian to invite her too. It couldn't be over . . . it just couldn't.

But before Emma's visit, Lucy had her big gym competition. She was taking her Compulsory Grade Three – any gymnast who wanted to compete at Elite level needed to pass all of their Compulsories. But if Lucy wanted to make to the Academy she needed to do more than just pass. She had to come in the top two or three in the region, and qualify for the Nationals.

Ellie had seen her sister in small local competitions before, but this was the first time she'd watched her at a bigger event. She remembered all too well how nervous she'd been when she went for her Grade Three, and she'd been much older than Lucy. She'd started late on Grades, whereas Lucy would be one of the youngest there.

Dad drove them all to Exeter in the Land Rover. Lucy was so nervous that her normally bright cheeks were pale as milk. Her bouncing red curls were pulled back tight from her face. Ellie had painstakingly plaited them into a French braid that wrapped around the front of her face and then wound back into a bun on the top. The whole concoction was sprayed with nearly a whole bottle of hairspray to ensure it stayed in place (something Lucy's curls usually refused to do) and the effect was so severe it made her look quite different from the fun-loving little sister Ellie knew and loved. It made Ellie realise that Lucy was no longer just her little sister; she was turning into a serious and determined gymnast for whom this competition mattered as much as Euros selections did for Ellie.

'You'll be wonderful!' Ellie told her as they sat side by side, bouncing up and down along the country roads.

'But my bar and vault are so basic,' said Lucy, her eyes bright with anxiety and hope and ambition all mixed up together. 'And I don't have half of the moves the other girls will have.'

'You have something else,' said Ellie, putting her arm around her sister and remembering what Fran had said to her, the day she left for the Academy. 'Something more important than that. You have heart, and that makes your gymnastics beautiful.'

'She's right,' said Nancy, who was wedged up against a load of oyster baskets and a rusty old outboard motor in the back. 'It comes from your ballet, I reckon. That's your thing – your secret ingredient. Ellie, remember how Sasha told us to find our secret ingredients – and it turned out that rowing was mine?'

'Well, that doesn't exactly cheer me up,' said Lucy. 'You found your ingredient and then immediately gave up gym!'

'Ah, but if I could have found a way to put boats into gymnastics, I might still be at the Academy today,' said Nancy with a resigned shrug. '*You* can combine ballet and gym and the effect is gorgeous. You know, when you're on the floor I sort of forget I'm even watching gymnastics.'

'Is that a good thing?'

'Yes,' said Ellie. 'Sian Edwards once told me that gym is more than a sport – it's also an art form. The best gymnasts ensure it's both.'

'Anyway, with my lucky scrunchie on, you can't go wrong,' said Nancy.

Lucy patted her head happily. Her bun was held in place with a sea-green scrunchie that Nancy had owned since she was about five.

'I wore it to every single competition for years,' said Nancy. 'Back when I won everything. I once lost it down the back of the sofa and I refused to compete till Mum found it!'

Lucy giggled.

'I only stopped wearing it when the Academy squad leo changed colour and it didn't match any more,' said Nancy. Then she gave an exaggerated sigh. 'I swear that's when things started going downhill for me!'

'Maybe if you'd kept wearing the magic scrunchie you'd be off to Euros selections now,' said Ellie with a smile. 'Instead of preparing for racing gig season.'

'Yikes!' Nancy grimaced. 'In that case, keep that thing away from me!'

'The leo is lucky too,' said Ellie.

Lucy was wearing the leotard she herself had given to Ellie as an Academy good luck gift. She had saved up and bought it with her own money. She had given it with so much love that it seemed right that she should have it back now. It really suited her, too. The soft blues and silvers looked totally different next to her orange hair than they had beside Ellie's paler colouring. They made Lucy look like a mermaid.

'Are you sure I can have it?' Lucy said. 'I mean – doesn't it still fit you?'

'You know,' Ellie confessed. 'It actually doesn't. I think I've grown – just in the month since I've been here.'

'Seriously?' said Nancy. 'You still look pretty titchy to me!'

Ellie giggled at her tall best friend. 'We're not all sunflowers like you, Nancy. But Vivian reckoned I needed a bit more height for vault, so perhaps it's a good thing.'

'Clearly rowing is good for you!' said Nancy. 'I always said that it was the solution to pretty much everything!'

CHAPTER
Eighteen

It felt strange to Ellie to be going to a competition and not competing. In some ways it was a relief – there was no pressure on her – nobody looking at her, nothing to lose. On the other hand, watching the hopeful young gymnasts throwing their hearts and souls into bar, beam, vault and floor routines made her even more homesick for the gym than ever.

'Can you get gym-sick?' she asked Nancy.

'I certainly get sick of gymnastics!'

'I think I'm suffering from withdrawal symptoms,' sighed Ellie. 'When I see those girls doing tumble sequences or beam dismounts I feel like throwing this stupid boot in the bin, leaping over the barrier and doing it myself.'

'Not the greatest idea,' said Nancy. 'Look who's on the judging panel.'

Ellie followed the direction of Nancy's gaze and caught sight of Emma Bannerdown's short-cropped blonde head of hair. And sitting next to her – to Ellie's astonishment – was Vivian Ponting. Like all the other judges she was dressed in a white shirt and black trousers, but somehow she made hers look like an army uniform. With her broad shoulders, slim hips and her shirt buttoned up to her chin she looked more terrifying even than Ellie had remembered her.

'She's judging vault, of course,' said Nancy. 'But what's she doing at a little local comp like this?'

'I guess if she's Junior GB squad coach she's on the lookout for new talents coming up through the ranks,' suggested Ellie.

'So long as they're not called Trengilly!' said Nancy.

Ellie sighed. She couldn't help feeling that if

Vivian didn't like her because of Lizzie, Lucy wasn't likely to fare any better. 'Let's hope she doesn't mark Lucy down just for being my sister!'

But Ellie needn't have worried. Lucy did brilliantly, easily passing the Grade and winning the bronze medal along the way. She was really turning into a very accomplished gymnast, particularly on the floor. She topped the competition there by two whole marks, making up for her weaker performance on vault and bar. Ellie clapped so hard that if her palms hadn't become tough and leathery from gigging they'd have been red raw.

Emma caught up with them on their way out. 'Hello Ellie, Nancy. I thought I might see you here.'

Ellie could feel the Academy head coach looking her up and down. She wished more than ever that she wasn't wearing the silly boot.

'Nancy, I swear you've grown again!' laughed Emma. 'It looks as if ocean-going life agrees with you.'

'Oh, it's a million times more fun here than the Academy,' said Nancy, then she added quickly, 'I mean – no offence, of course.'

'None taken,' laughed Emma. 'And what about you, Ellie? How's the change of scene suiting you?'

'It's nice to be home,' said Ellie. 'But I just want to get back to the Academy and proper training as soon as possible.'

'Well, I'm going to swing by tomorrow to see how you're getting on,' said Emma. 'You've got a hospital appointment in the morning, right? We'll see how you're looking after that.'

'We?' asked Ellie.

'Vivian's coming too,' said Emma, matter-of-factly.

'Oh.' Ellie nodded, her heart fluttering with a mixture of fear and excitement. Then she added quickly, 'I've been working really hard, keeping up with every bit of conditioning I can possibly manage.'

'Without putting undue stress on that foot, I hope?' said Emma.

'No – I've been so careful.'

'You certainly look well,' said Emma, looking her up and down. 'I do believe you may have grown a little too, Ellie Trengilly.'

'I have.'

'You've got a bit of colour in those pasty white cheeks too!' said a loud Aussie voice. Ellie turned round to see Vivian standing behind her. How long had she been listening to the conversation? 'And a bit more meat on your scrawny bones.'

Ellie flushed. 'I guess that's Langer.'

'Yes, I heard he was working you hard.' Vivian raised an eyebrow but Ellie couldn't figure out what she was thinking. At that moment, Lucy came bounding out of the changing room, barging past Emma and Vivian as she flung herself at Ellie, breathless with excitement. 'It worked – the leo worked – and the scrunchie. I got a bit of your magic from it, I could feel it!'

'This must be your little sister, Lucy,' said Emma with a smile.

Lucy turned and realised who she had just barged past. She went bright red and stuttered, 'I'm sorry – I . . . I . . .'

'You were very good today,' said Emma kindly, seeing her confusion. 'I particularly enjoyed your floor routine. It was very elegant.'

Lucy seemed suddenly incapable of speech.

Vivian regarded the two sisters with her cool gaze.

'Lucy's just like Ellie,' said Nancy, stepping in. 'Don't you think?'

Emma's grey eyes narrowed. 'I could see a bit of Ellie in her,' she said. 'But she's a different sort of gymnast. Her own sort.'

'She was wonderful on the floor,' said Ellie. 'It's all the ballet she does, you see.'

'Yes,' said Emma. 'I could see that.'

'Your bar work lets you down,' said Vivian bluntly. 'And your vault's not as strong as it could be either. That's something you have in common with your sister.'

Lucy's face fell and Ellie wanted to scream at the coach – not for getting at her, but for upsetting her little sister.

Nancy stepped in. 'Come on, guys,' she said with forced cheeriness. 'We'd better be going. Your dad'll be waiting.'

'See you both tomorrow,' said Emma.

'Both?' asked Lucy, flushing again in confusion.

'Yes,' said Emma, her grey eyes smiling. 'I'm looking forward to seeing *both* of you!'

'She said you looked well,' said Nancy when they all reached home that night. Mum had laid on a special celebratory supper for Lucy, but she and Ellie had both been too nervous to really enjoy it. The prospect of Vivian and Emma coming to check them out in the gym the next day was nearly as nerve-wracking as the competition itself. It meant everything to Ellie. Could she still have a shot at being invited for the selection weekend?

'Yes, but a suntan's not going to get me to selections,' Ellie sighed. 'I need to prove to her that I'm fully recovered – and that I haven't *lost* ground in the meantime.'

'Are you?' asked Nancy.

'Am I what?'

'Fully recovered?'

'Of course I am,' said Ellie. 'My ankle hardly bothers me at all any more.'

It was true. Ellie's ankle felt a million times better than it had when she'd first been sent home.

'If they'd just let me get back to normal training I might still have time to prepare for Euros – there are still two weeks to go before the selection weekend.'

'I can't decide if I want you to do well or not,' said Nancy, stretching out on her camp bed and wiggling her toes. 'I'm almost tempted to put itching powder in both your beds – or a banana skin under the beam – you know, so you both mess up tomorrow.'

Ellie laughed. 'You sound like Scarlett!'

'If you get the all-clear from the doc, you'll be back at the Academy so quick we won't see you for dust,' said Nancy. 'And Lucy won't be far behind – then where will that leave me? All alone in the creek with your mum's cooking and Langer's death-by-rowing regime!'

'Which you love,' Ellie pointed out.

'I do – but it's much more fun with you in the boat.'

Ellie laughed. 'I love spending time with you and Lucy. And I've even kind of enjoyed the rowing,' she admitted. 'But I have to get back to normal training to even stand a chance of getting to selections.'

'I get it,' said Nancy. 'What's that thing they say? If you love something, let it go. But don't expect me to be happy about waving you off!'

Ellie lay in bed and wiggled her own toes. Her ankle still ached a tiny bit, but that was only to be expected, wasn't it? It felt so much better – almost back to normal. But would it be strong enough for her to start full training again? For her to stand a chance of getting invited along to Euros selections?

Only tomorrow would tell.

CHAPTER
Nineteen

Ellie went to the hospital first thing the next morning. Her foot was X-rayed and pronounced, 'Much improved.'

'What does that mean?'

'It means the fracture has virtually healed,' the doctor told her. He was a grey-haired Cornish man with a matter-of-fact manner. 'It's mended far quicker than we expected. The Cornish air must have worked its magic on these bones of yours.'

Ellie felt her heart soar.

'So I can take the boot off?'

'Yes,' he said with a smile.

'And get back to full training again?'

The doctor frowned. 'It will still be vulnerable for the next six weeks or so. Normally we would advise against any impact sport in that time.'

'But this isn't *normal*,' said Nancy. The whole family had come along to the appointment and they were all squeezed into the doctor's office as he gave his verdict. 'Ellie's an elite athlete. GB squad. She wants to go to European Championships.'

'She *needs* to go!' added Lucy. 'If she wants to get to the Olympics next year, that is.'

The doctor smiled. 'I see. Well, I'd advise a phased return to training. Keeping to soft surfaces and minimising impact landings as far as possible to start with.'

'But you think I can do it?'

'If you take it slowly and carefully . . .'

Ellie jumped up and nearly hugged him, stopping herself just in time. 'I'm sorry! It's just the best thing EVER!'

'Glad to be the bearer of good news,' said the doctor. 'But don't expect things to go back to normal right away.'

Ellie sighed. She knew he was right. The boot might be coming off, but she now had a race against time to get back up to full fitness before the selection weekend. If only she was allowed back to the Academy now, she might just stand a chance . . .

Ellie was still buzzing as the girls made their way to the gym, but when they got there Vivian quickly managed to put a damper on her good mood.

Emma was with Lucy, helping her with a new bar technique she was trying to master and discussing her progress with Fran, while Vivian worked with Ellie.

She looked at the X-rays and the doctor's notes in silence, then watched as Ellie worked her way through the training regimen she'd sent through for the week. Ellie expected her to be as critical as she had been at National squad camp, but Vivian hardly said anything. She made a lot of notes and asked Ellie a few questions, and that was about it. It was strange working without the boot on and Ellie was surprised to find she missed the sense of safety it gave her. Without it she felt nervous suddenly, wary of putting weight on her bad foot – even though the doctor had said it was healed.

She knew her balance had improved from all the one-legged work she'd been doing, and she knew she was stronger from the gigging. But when Vivian didn't comment on anything, good or bad, Ellie couldn't figure out whether her silence was encouraging – or just the opposite.

As they worked she found herself thinking about Vivian and Lizzie. People were always telling Ellie that she looked just like Lizzie. Is that what Vivian saw when she looked at her? Lucy had read an interview in which Vivian had been asked if her rivalry with Lizzie was a friendly one. 'There's no such thing as a *friendly* rivalry!' Vivian had responded.

By the time the session came to an end, Ellie still couldn't work out what Vivian thought. The three coaches went off to the office whilst Ellie, Lucy and Nancy sat in the changing room, waiting for the verdict.

'I feel like a criminal waiting to find out if I've been sentenced,' said Ellie.

'But you said she was all right,' said Lucy. That's got to be a good sign, right?'

'I didn't say *all right*,' said Ellie. 'She just didn't say much.'

'It's pretty much the same thing for Vivian,' said Nancy, who had watched the whole session from the viewing window.

'Maybe,' said Ellie. 'Hey, Emma must think a lot of you, Lucy, to spend so much time with you.'

'I don't know,' said Lucy, flushing. 'She saw me trying to do lots of stuff I haven't mastered yet. But she gave me great tips on the bar, and I nearly managed to nail a new skill.'

'Oh - here they come!' said Nancy, jumping up excitedly.

But as the three coaches emerged from the office, Ellie could tell straight away that it wasn't good news.

'We think that you should stay here for a bit longer,' Emma said.

Ellie could barely take in what she was being told. 'But my foot is healed - the doctor said - I can gradually get back to full training.'

'Yes, I know,' said Emma. 'But Vivian thinks you're not ready yet.'

'Vivian thinks!' Ellie managed to stammer. She wanted to scream, to shout, to throw her gym bag across the room, but she could barely get out the two words.

'She thinks you'll benefit from spending more time with your family and working on your rowing.'

'But she can't row her way to Euros,' said Nancy. 'Not that she's not good enough to row – she's fab, as it happens.'

'Yeah, Langer told me you were making good progress,' said Vivian. Ellie stared at her with eyes full of tears and anger, and Vivian met them with a cool, unshaken expression of her own.

'Vivian's devised a full programme for you to work on here,' said Fran gently, sensing Ellie's acute distress. 'So you'll gradually get back full mobility in your injured leg.'

'You've been carrying around the extra weight of the boot on the bad leg,' Emma explained. 'Which means the muscles have had to overcompensate.'

'It's not as bad as it could have been,' said Vivian. 'Langer making you row only on your good leg has almost balanced it out.'

'Almost . . .' whispered Ellie. 'But when can I come back to the Academy?'

'We'll just see how it goes,' said Vivian.

'And what about the selection weekend?' asked Nancy. 'Can she go to that?'

'I'll make a decision nearer the time,' said Vivian.

Ellie barely heard what was said after that. She had been as high as a kite after the visit to the hospital, but now she came crashing down to earth. Arrangements for her ongoing training regime were being made, but she scarcely listened. She only heard what Emma said to Lucy as she left: 'I look forward to seeing how you get on at National Grade finals, young lady. I'll keep an eye out for you, OK?'

Lucy was flushing and looking happier than Ellie had ever seen her.

But Ellie had never felt so miserable.

CHAPTER
Twenty

For the next week and a half, Ellie went about in a daze.

'It's not the end of the road,' Tam had said when they'd Skyped one night. He'd also had a call-back for the boys' squad selection weekend. Ellie could tell he felt terrible – but now she was the only one who didn't yet know her fate.

'My foot's fully healed. I'm back working on a full training programme but still she doesn't want me to go back to the Academy. There's no way I'll be invited to the selection weekend now. She might as well have kicked me out of GB squad there and then.'

'I can't believe Emma would go along with this if Vivian's just being spiteful,' said Nancy with a puzzled expression.

'Exactly,' said Katya. 'Maybe there is a top-secret plan you is not knowing about.'

'A plan to end my gym career,' said Ellie gloomily. And no matter how hard the others tried to cheer her up, nothing worked.

The only place where she could forget her worries for a bit was out on the gig. Now that she had both legs working, she could keep up with the pace of the rest of the crew easily and she was surprised by how much she loved it. The summer was out in full force now, blazing-hot sunshine and cloudless skies that made it glorious to be out on the water. The beaches were rammed with tourists and there were boats of every variety on the waves – sailors, kayakers, paddleboards, motorboats, giant yachts and even big tankers, stretched out on the horizon like toy battleships.

Ellie knew that she was looking healthier. Her pale face was covered in freckles and her hair was taking on a sun-kissed shine. And it was surprisingly exhilarating to think that she was now a strong member of the gigging team, rather than its weakest link.

'I'm not sure we want Matthew Jones back!' Nancy declared a week after Vivian's disastrous visit to the gym. 'I swear you're better than he is now!'

'It's a good job too,' said Charlie. 'We've got the Falmouth gig race this weekend, and Matt's only just out of plaster.'

'Are you looking forward to it?' Nancy asked. 'I mean, I know you weren't exactly planning to still be here for race season, but still . . .'

Ellie tried her best to look excited. 'You know, I actually am,' she said. 'It's just a bit weird because . . .'

'Because Saturday is the start of Euros selection weekend,' Nancy finished her sentence for her.

Ellie nodded.

'And you'd rather be there.'

Ellie shrugged. 'But since I obviously won't, it's good to be busy and keep my mind off it.'

'Oh, we'll be lucky if Langer gives us a chance to

155

breathe, let alone think!' laughed Nancy.

And she was right. Training for the Falmouth event meant lots of practice off the shipwreck beach where, at low tide, they finally got to see the giant rusty hull resting on the ocean floor near the rocks.

'It's so awesome!' Nancy yelled back to Ellie as they rowed past it. 'Like a giant sea-dragon, fast asleep.'

'I always think of the sailors who were on board when she went down,' Ellie yelled back. 'Do you think anyone survived?'

'There's a lifeboat station just along the coast,' said Nancy. 'They'd have come out in time to rescue them, right?'

Ellie shrugged. 'I asked Dad and he reckons that the year it went down they still had lifeboats with oars, not modern speedboats.'

'A bit like a gig, then?' said Nancy.

'Exactly like a gig.'

They rowed on round the coastline, passing a couple of kayakers who had set up camp on one of the little beaches that appeared only at low tide. The sun was still high in the sky but on the horizon a grey storm cloud loomed ominously.

'What's the betting we get a soaking by the end of the session?' Nancy asked.

She was right. For the first half of the training session the sun shone brightly, but as they began to make their way back along the coast the first drops of rain started to fall. The tide had turned and the little beaches were now all disappearing, submerged beneath the waves until the next ebb tide. The sun had vanished and the sky was grey and heavy as they neared the shipwreck beach. As the rain battered down and the wind whipped up little squalls on the waves, rowing became harder than ever.

'The forecast for race day is even worse than this,' Langer yelled over the barrage of rain. 'So you might as well get used to it.'

It was hard to see where they were going through the torrent. They had to rely on the calls from Langer to keep them clear of the rocks. Above the hammering of the rain and the crash of the waves it was only just possible to hear Langer's voice but after a while Ellie became dimly aware of another noise, a high-pitched cry like that of an animal in distress.

'Did you hear that?' she shouted at Nancy.

'What?'

Ellie strained her ears. There it was again. A desperate seagull-like call, but more frantic, like a baby crying in terror.

'There.'

Nancy had heard it now and so had the others.

'Stop!' cried Joe. 'Look over there!'

Dimly, peering through the rain, they saw where he was pointing. In one of the inlets where earlier they'd seen the kayakers lounging on the temporary beach, they saw the same two figures – a man and a little boy. Only now the beach was gone and it looked like they were stranded.

'The tide must have come in too quickly,' shouted Nancy. 'And now they can't get out of the cove.'

The two figures were standing on a rock in the middle of the inlet, but the waves were crashing all around them and the tide was coming in fast. Even their temporary refuge would be underwater soon.

'We have to do something!' shouted Ellie.

They had all stopped rowing and the gig was bouncing on the swell of the waves, drenching them with every smack and fall.

'The lifeboat will be here soon,' shouted Charlie.

The two figures on the rock had spotted the gig and were waving frantically, shouting at the tops of their voices.

'It could be too late by then,' said Nancy. 'The tide comes in really fast here, remember?'

'We can't just leave them!' said Ellie, looking desperately around at the others.

'Too right,' said Langer.

Ellie remembered what Lucy had said about how gigs had been used as lifeboats once upon a time. But the waves were frothing around the inlet like a cauldron and the kayakers were surrounded by jagged rocks that could rip the gig apart.

'Here's the plan,' said Langer. 'We row in there, bundle them on board. It won't be easy to row with the extra cargo, but it can be done. I don't see any other way.'

'But what about those rocks?' asked Charlie. 'We could be smashed to pieces!'

'Then we just have to avoid them!' yelled Langer. 'Come on. Let's turn her about. We need to be quick. They're nearly submerged already.'

It was hard work turning the gig about. It seemed like complete madness, sending this small, flimsy boat into the jaws of the foaming inlet. The rain continued to fall mercilessly and the clouds were so dark that it felt like evening. But Ellie tried to push all that out of her mind and just concentrate on the strokes, on following Langer's voice as they skirted perilously close to the giant rocks at the mouth of the cove. Ellie felt the boat lurch and stifled a scream. Panicking now wasn't going to help anyone.

As they drew closer to the two kayakers, they could see that the boy was only about six years old. He was terrified, clinging to his dad as the waves lapped up around his ankles. Ellie's heart swelled with sympathy. Their kayak was lodged into a nearby ravine – it had been ripped by the swell.

'How do we get close enough to get them on board?' yelled Nancy.

'I haven't figured that bit out yet!' said Langer.

For a moment Ellie allowed herself to think what could happen if the gig was smashed on to the rocks. Her head filled with visions of broken limbs, a cracked skull, torn ligaments. They were injuries that would put her out of gymnastics for ever – and that's if she didn't drown. But then she looked at the boy's frightened face and pushed all that out of her mind. They had to save him – they just had to.

They were battling against the currents and the swell of the waves just to stay still. Ellie felt her shoulders screaming in pain, and her ankle too. She had to jam her whole foot hard against the board to try and steady herself and she could feel an agonising hot pain that she daren't even think about.

'We need to time it just right,' shouted Langer. 'We wait for a big wave to take us forwards, then we get them on board before the swell goes out again. If we get it wrong, we'll pull them into the water and capsize the gig at the same time.'

He waved madly at the father, trying to communicate this. The man yelled something back, but his words were lost in the crash of wind and rain.

'We've just got to go for it,' Langer shouted to the crew at last. 'On the next swell we all heave forwards, OK?'

Ellie could see that they were running out of time. The rock on which the kayakers were perched was almost underwater now and the little boy was shivering with terror.

'Everyone ready?' Langer yelled.

With the next surge of wave they gave a heave on the oars, tipping them right alongside the rock. The boy was held out by his father, Langer grabbed hold of him and between them they bundled him on board. Then Langer reached for the man, but the tide was already tugging them backwards. Langer's arm was almost wrenched out of his socket as he clung on to the man. The stern of the boat was being dragged round by the swell and Ellie heard a sickening crunch as the bow smashed against the rock. The little boy was sobbing and as she pulled as hard as she could on the oars to steady them, her foot screamed once more in agony.

'Hold steady!' Langer yelled as, with a supreme effort, he managed to cling on to the rock and the dad scrambled into the gig. His additional weight almost overturned them, but the current was in their favour this time, pulling in the other direction so that they stayed upright.

'We need to turn her around!' Langer yelled. 'At oars. Now!'

But it wasn't that easy. With the extra weight on board and the current against them it felt almost impossible to get away from the rocks and out to the safety of open sea.

Ellie didn't think she'd ever been so frightened and in so much pain as she was for the next five minutes. It felt as if they were fighting a losing battle against the current, the boy was whimpering pitifully, the bow of the boat was damaged and she was convinced they were never going to get out alive.

But if gymnastics had taught Ellie anything, it

was to never give up. She knew how to keep her body working, even when every muscle screamed against it. And, thanks to Langer's 'pain is power' training regime, so did the rest of the team. He had hold of Nancy's oar and between them they were making headway, getting free of the treacherous swell and current.

They were nearly round the rocks now and free from immediate danger. But they were tiring and it was still a fair distance round to the safety of the beach beyond the headland.

'Not much further now!' Langer yelled.

And that's when Ellie saw the most welcome sight in the world. Powering across the waves, a vision of orange and flashing lights, was the lifeboat.

'Here come the cavalry!' Nancy managed to shout through the wind and rain. The little boy stopped crying for the first time.

Ellie didn't think she'd ever felt so grateful to see a lifeboat. The larger vessel drew level with theirs, and before she knew it the boy and his father were being bundled out, followed by the gig crew members.

'We can't leave the boat,' Nancy was saying. 'We've got races coming up!'

'We'll tow her ashore,' the lifeboat man yelled back. 'You've done enough here already. We don't want another emergency on our hands.'

So Nancy reluctantly handed over her oar and let herself be dragged up into the lifeboat. Langer was last to leave the gig. Before he did, he and the lifeboat men secured her to the bigger vessel. And then they were off, powering across the waves, away from the perilous rocks, towards safety.

The small boy was in his father's arms, sobbing with relief. The dad just looked shocked. 'I can't thank you enough,' he kept saying. 'You saved our lives. You saved our lives.'

'The lifeboat was on its way,' said Langer.

'We wouldn't have made it on time,' said the captain. 'He's right enough. You saved their lives – even if it was a pretty stupid thing to do.'

Ellie sat in the back of the boat, suddenly exhausted and numb, even though her body was in agony. The enormity of what had just happened was starting to hit her – the inlet, the current sucking them towards the rocks. She knew they were lucky – incredibly lucky – to have got out in one piece. And yet, she was also aware of her foot, throbbing like it had when she'd first hurt it. Had she just blown her Euros chances once and for all?

CHAPTER
Twenty-One

Back at the lifeboat station they were bundled into blankets, plied with hot chocolate and biscuits and checked over for shock.

'Totally mad thing to do,' the lifeboat quartermaster kept telling them. 'But you saved that little boy's life, no doubt about it.'

The little boy – whose name, as he kept telling everyone, was Sydney Arthur Alexander Donlan – had overcome his fear and was now racing round the lifeboat station, demanding to be shown every bit of kit they owned. 'He doesn't seem to be in shock, does he?' Nancy commented.

'Crew, you were amazing,' said Langer once they'd all been checked over. 'I don't care how we do in the race season, I have never – and I mean never – been prouder of a crew of men than I was today.'

'Even though two of us are girls?' asked Nancy.

'Probably *because* two of you are girls!' Langer laughed. 'It was a team effort, but we definitely couldn't have saved the day without a bit of girl power.'

Dad and Lucy picked them up from the lifeboat station. 'It's all over the local radio,' Lucy squeaked excitedly. 'You're heroines!'

'She's right,' said Dad. 'The newspaper wants to interview you and everything.'

'Fame at last!' announced Nancy, gleefully. 'Forget winning gold medals, acts of bravery and heroism on the sea are the way to do it!'

'I might have to forget about gold medals,' said Ellie, as the Land Rover made its way along the winding lanes. The rain danced like crystals through its headlights. 'I think I've hurt my ankle again.'

'No!' said Nancy. 'How?'

'Rowing the gig today,' said Ellie, gazing out into the gloom, feeling despair wash over her now the excitement of the day had worn off. 'I was putting too much pressure on it, I guess.'

'Do you – do you think the fracture's opened up again?' Lucy asked. Ellie was afraid to hear the answer from the others in the car.

'Let's hope not, sweetie. But try not to worry – we'll get you checked out first thing tomorrow,' said Dad. 'In the meantime, if I don't get you home pronto your mum'll probably call out search and rescue herself!'

'I'm sure it's going to be OK,' whispered Nancy, leaning in close and hugging her friend.

Ellie said nothing, just stared out of the Land Rover as the sun set over the sea, which was now calm as a millpond again.

When they called Tam and Katya that evening, the pair of them were agog. 'You are like superheroes!' said Katya. 'But I am always saying boats are very dangerous.'

'For once, Katya, you're right,' said Nancy. 'Even I didn't much enjoy today's session – well, the bit when we got rescued and treated like heroes and force-fed chocolate biscuits for the shock was good, but the nearly-being-dashed-to-pieces-on-the-rocks bit I was less keen on!'

The Academy gymnasts were all packing to go to the National Sports Training Centre for the selection weekend the following day, Friday. 'Have you heard anything yet?' Tam asked Ellie.

Ellie shook her head. In her heart of hearts she'd been clinging on to the hope that she might get a last minute call-up. But she'd heard nothing, and now she couldn't help feeling desperately disappointed.

'Emma said she had a big surprise waiting for us when we got to the National Sports Training Centre,' said Tam. 'We were kind of hoping it was going to be you.'

Ellie shrugged. 'No such luck, I'm afraid.'

'What can the surprise be, then?' asked Lucy. Ellie knew Lucy was trying to change the subject for her sake, and she was grateful.

'Ooh – perhaps Vivian has left and gone back to Australia!' said Nancy hopefully.

Ellie sighed. 'Promise me you'll Skype and tell us?' she asked. 'And you both have to do your very best to make that Euros squad. I want the Academy to be represented!'

CHAPTER
Twenty-Two

Ellie had been terrified about her ankle. But when she went to see the doctor on Friday, there was good news. 'The fracture's healed fine,' he said. 'Just a bit of bruising here. And probably a case of crystal foot syndrome.'

'What's that?' asked Ellie, alarmed.

'Well, after a broken bone heals it's normal to be excessively fearful about it happening again,' he explained. 'You feel like the limb is made of glass and might shatter at any time.'

'But it won't?'

'No,' the doctor smiled. 'Your adventure of

yesterday doesn't seem to have done you any harm at all.'

'That's brilliant news!' said Lucy.

And there was even more good news waiting for Ellie when she got home.

'You had a phone call,' said Mum, who was in one of her painting moods and so even scattier than usual. She had a large blob of orange paint on her nose, and a paintbrush sticking out of her headscarf at a very odd angle.

'Um – did they leave a message?' asked Ellie. 'Or say who they were?'

'She was called Iron, I think.' Mum scratched her nose, spreading the orange blob alarmingly.

'Iron?' Lucy asked, puzzled.

'Or Copper . . . maybe Brass . . . It was definitely a metal name. Let me think . . .'

'Steele,' suggested Nancy helpfully.

'Yes, that's it. Barbara Steele. I knew it'd come to me.' Mum grinned, her orange nose wrinkling happily.

'She's only the GB head coach, Mum!' said Lucy.

It was sometimes hard to believe how little Mum knew about gymnastics, despite having two gym-mad daughters. 'What did she say? Please say you haven't forgotten that as well!'

'Oh, dear me – didn't I tell you?' said Mum, who seemed dreamily unaware that this was a big deal. 'She wants Ellie to go up to the National Sports Training Centre for some kind of camp. She mentioned . . . selections?'

'Euros selections?' squeaked Nancy.

'Hmm!' said Mum who had a faraway expression on her face. 'Yes, I think that might have been it.'

'Are you serious?' asked Lucy.

Ellie was too shocked to say anything.

'Yes, now that I think about it, I'm quite sure that's what she said. I even wrote it down somewhere – although I can't for the life of me remember where!'

'Mum, you're the worst!' groaned Lucy.

'Look!' yelled Nancy. 'Here it is. You stuck a note on the toaster – *Barbara Steele wants Ellie to go to Euros selections. Tomorrow.*'

Ellie stared at the note, barely able to read the words properly.

'I remember now!' said Mum, brightening as if a light bulb had switched on in her head. 'This Barbara lady had heard about your lifesaving adventure and said she thought she'd better get you back safely in a gym before you did any more daring deeds.'

'I . . . I can't believe it,' Ellie managed to stammer.

'Epic!' shrieked Lucy, and then her face fell. 'Oh, but we're going to miss you so much.'

'We'll miss you at the Falmouth gig race tomorrow too,' said Nancy, ruefully.

Ellie, whose head had been in the clouds, suddenly came back down to earth.

'Oh, Nancy, I didn't think. I . . . I mean, I could delay going,' said Ellie suddenly. She was surprised to hear the words coming out of her mouth, but she realised that she meant it. 'I would, you know.'

'No way are you missing Euros selections!' said Nancy.

'But I don't want to let you down.'

'Don't stress about us!' grinned Nancy. 'I have a cunning plan.'

'Which is?' asked Lucy, curiously.

'Top secret!' said Nancy with a smile. 'Now let's go help you pack, Miss Gymnastic-Fantastic! What would be the best leo for Euros, do y'reckon?'

The next few hours were a whirl of preparations and goodbyes. Dad was driving Ellie up to the National Sports Training Centre at the crack of dawn on Saturday. It was only when she was climbing into the Land Rover in the misty morning light that Ellie realised just how sad she was to leave the creek. She hadn't wanted to come home – she'd spent her whole time in Cornwall wanting to be in London or at the National Sports Training Centre – but as she looked out at the shimmering waters of the creek, she knew that it wasn't just her ankle that had healed. She felt more relaxed than she had in ages, more herself somehow.

And she'd also discovered that she wasn't irreplaceable. Her spot on the gig team had already been filled. Matt Jones was out of plaster but not yet ready to row, so Nancy had persuaded Langer to give Lucy a try-out.

'Just until Matt's back on form,' Lucy explained over dinner, looking shy but pleased at her sudden promotion.

'Langer's finally decided that gymnasts are a good bet,' Nancy grinned. 'Although he says he's not investing any time in one who's just about to swan off to London.'

'But I'm not,' said Lucy quickly.

'You never know,' said Ellie. 'You heard what Emma said. She'll be watching out for you at Nationals.'

'She also said I need to work on my bar and vault,' Lucy reminded her.

'Yes, and look how much more muscly Ellie's arms have become since she started gigging,' said Nancy. 'The same could happen to you now you're on five!'

Ellie glanced down at her arms. She had to admit that Nancy was right. She would never be

177

a powerhouse like Memory Danster, but her arms didn't look quite so much like a pair of strawberry laces as they had before she began to row.

'Maybe that was Vivian's plan all along,' said Nancy.

'Hmm . . .' said Ellie. She hadn't failed to notice that it had been Barbara who had rung to invite her to the selection weekend, not Vivian. 'Maybe.'

The drive took several hours, and as they sat side by side in the Land Rover, Dad entertained Ellie with stories of Lizzie's time at National squad camps when they were kids. It was so nice to hear him talk about Lizzie, instead of changing the subject every time Ellie'd tried to talk about her, the way he had been doing recently, although it made Ellie even more desperate to get to know her aunt than ever.

'She and Emma and Fran used to have midnight feasts and sneak out to meet boys from the rugby team!' Dad laughed. 'I used to think it sounded like something out of one of those boarding school stories.'

'Emma Bannerdown broke the rules and snuck out at night?' said Ellie in astonishment.

'Oh, she was the ringleader, apparently!' said Dad. 'Not that your aunt was an angel. I think Fran tried to exert a good influence over them, but the other two dragged her into their scrapes.'

Ellie giggled. 'Emma's always going on about gymnastics needing absolute dedication!'

'Oh, I think they worked very hard – but they played hard too,' said Dad. As he said that, they turned up the long driveway to the National Sports Training Centre. Ellie felt even more excited than she had the first time she'd come. 'You'll see . . .'

'What do you mean?'

Dad grinned and tapped his nose mysteriously. Ellie realised that he'd been acting strangely since she got the call-up yesterday, like he knew some big secret. 'Ask me no questions and I'll tell you no lies,' he said cryptically.

'What does that even mean?'

They were nearly at the top of the long avenue of trees now and Ellie caught her first glimpse of the grand old house, its soft yellow stone glowing in the early-morning sunshine. Her heart soared and she felt as if her insides were doing a giant on the bar.

'It means we're here,' said Dad. 'So let's get you reunited with your friends. I bet they're dying to see you.'

The other Academy gymnasts who'd been selected had all arrived the night before – boys and girls, Seniors and Juniors had all come up together from London in the minibus . Ellie could hardly wait to see them either. Well, most of them!

'They are – but I bet Scarlett isn't!' said Ellie with a grin. 'Nancy reckons she was gutted when she heard I was coming back. Ooh. I wonder if they've found out what Emma's big news is yet?'

'Oh, I think you'll find out soon enough!' said Dad with a laugh.

CHAPTER
Twenty-Three

Ellie found everyone eating breakfast picnic-style in the garden in front of the big house. Tam and some of the other boys were kicking a ball around whilst they munched on toast, and Katya was walking along the wall on her hands. Sian Edwards was talking to Bella and Sophia, while Scarlett was lying on a blanket, sipping a smoothie and wearing a giant pair of movie-star sunglasses. Ellie stood for a second looking at them all. Then Tam caught sight of Ellie, ditched the ball and sprinted up the steps two at a time.

'Hey – Trengilly – what took you so long?'

He picked her up in a giant hug and swung her round, ignoring the wolf-whistles and cheers from the other boys. Ellie found herself going pink. Then Katya came and flung herself at Ellie so hard they she nearly did them both an injury.

'Ellie!' she squealed. 'You are all spotty.'

'I hope you mean freckly!' laughed Ellie, recovering her composure. 'It's fab to see you all!'

'You too, kiddo!' said Sian, who had also come up to greet her. 'You look really well. How are you feeling?'

'My ankle's much better,' said Ellie. 'But I've only been back to a full training schedule for a week or two. I couldn't believe it when I got the call.'

'Vivian came to see you, didn't she?' asked Sian. 'She must think you're up to it.'

Ellie sighed at the mention of Vivian. 'I'm not sure what she thinks of me any more, to be honest.'

'Forget about that for a moment,' said Katya, who was bouncing around like a toy on springs. 'We have best surprise for you!'

'Um – what?'

'No questions,' laughed Tam. 'She's right. You have to come to the gym *right* now!'

'But I haven't even dropped my bags in my room,' said Ellie, as the others clustered round her and started dragging her in the direction of the gym. 'I didn't think we were training till nine.'

The others were all looking at each other with shining eyes. Ellie couldn't figure out what was going on.

'Oh, stop talking and just do as you're told for once, Trengilly!' said Tam.

Ellie laughed. 'You sound just like Langer!'

She gave in and let the others drag her up the steps, through the archway, past the lions and all the way to the door of the gym. Then they all stopped.

'You should go in on your own,' said Tam. He looked suddenly serious and the others had gone quiet. Ellie felt more confused than ever.

'He's right,' said Bella. 'We'll wait out here.'

'I – I still don't get it.'

'You will,' said Tam. 'Go on.'

Still feeling puzzled, Ellie pushed open the door of the gym and stood in the shadows at its edge. The slanting morning light cast a golden glow across the blue practice floor that reminded Ellie of the shining surface of the creek. At first she thought the gym was empty, but then she noticed a solitary gymnast working on the floor. The girl wore an old practice leotard and faded leggings. There was no music playing, but she was obviously working though the steps of a routine. It was like a silent movie – Ellie felt as if she could almost hear the music in the air, a haunting strain running through the shafts of sunlight round the gymnast's body.

The gymnast seemed to float, swim almost through the air, and Ellie felt as if she was watching a ghost. She'd often imagined the great gymnasts who had danced their way across this floor over the years, wondered if their spirits lingered in the high vaulted ceilings of the gym. But this gymnast was no phantom. The floor vibrated as she landed, and Ellie could hear her breaths coming fast. There was something about the way she moved that was strangely familiar. As the gymnast turned for her final tumble sequence, Ellie saw her face reflected for a split second in a mirror, before she launched into a powerful round-off flick straight back with a full twist and straight into a split leap. She spun, spun, leapt then sank into a final pose. Then she looked up with a breathless laugh and Ellie saw her face properly for the first time.

Ellie, hidden in the shadows, caught her breath at the sight.

'How was that?' the gymnast asked.

'Better, Liz, but seriously – that final pirouette is totally off.'

Ellie, still barely able to breathe, became suddenly aware of a second figure standing in the corner.

'You are the meanest coach in the world, Viv,' smiled the gymnast, getting up from the floor with laughter still in her voice. 'You do know that, right?'

'You know what they say – if you want a coach who's going to go easy on you, don't pick your former rival.'

'Oh, I forgot. Silly me. They do say that, don't they.'

A single word slipped out of Ellie's mouth. 'Lizzie?' She'd stared at that face in her gym books so often – and it was so like her own – that she could hardly mistake it. There, standing in the middle of the blue sprung floor, in an old black practice leo and a tatty pair of leggings, was Lizzie Trengilly. Aunt Lizzie.

CHAPTER
Twenty-Four

'I don't understand. I thought you were . . . I didn't know where you were . . .'

Ellie was sitting in the middle of the floor with Vivian Ponting and Lizzie Trengilly on either side of her. The gym was still empty apart from the three of them. It felt like time had stood still.

'Here,' said Vivian, handing her a bottle of water. 'Drink this. You look like you've seen a ghost.'

Ellie said nothing, just glanced from one to the other. It felt as though the spirits of two former gymnasts had come uncannily to life before her eyes.

'I've been here all along,' Lizzie said. Even the

way she sat, one leg tucked under the other, looked elegant somehow.

'Here?' said Ellie. She couldn't help feeling a twinge of sadness, betrayal and disappointment. Lizzie had been here, in England, at the National Sports Training Centre. She could have been in touch, could have at least let Ellie know. 'But – you said you had a new project.'

'Yes. This is it,' said Lizzie.

'Lizzie decided not to keep coaching,' Vivian explained. 'She's coming back to competing instead.'

Ellie felt almost as if she was dreaming. None of this made any sense. 'But your leg . . .'

'I saw a specialist in America,' Lizzie explained gently. She was looking at Ellie the way Dad looked at her sometimes. 'He's developed an experimental form of surgery. It was a risk, but it worked. I'm sorry I didn't tell you, but I needed to keep it to myself until I knew for certain.'

'Knew *what* for certain?'

'Whether I could ever compete again.'

Ellie was struggling to keep up with all the

new information. 'You mean . . .'

'Lizzie came here so she could use the facilities at the rehabilitation centre,' Vivian explained. 'I believe you know it?'

She raised an eyebrow as she said this and Ellie flushed. It seemed that Vivian Ponting knew everything.

'She's been working with Sam and some of the physios,' Vivian went on. 'Getting herself back to full fitness.'

'And Vivian's been coaching me,' added Lizzie with a smile.

'But . . .' said Ellie, her astonishment growing with each new revelation. 'But I thought you hated each other!'

Both Vivian and Lizzie laughed. 'It's true we weren't always the best of friends,' said Lizzie. 'But I wouldn't exactly say we hated each other.'

Vivian shrugged. 'Speak for yourself, Trengilly,' she said with a grin. 'I pretty much loathed your guts. Seriously, I swore that if you robbed me of one more gold medal I was gonna strangle you!'

'But . . . I don't understand,' said Ellie. 'Why would you want to help her now?'

Lizzie glanced at Vivian and a silent look of agreement seemed to pass between them. 'I always felt it was my fault – that Lizzie was hurt,' Vivian said, her face more serious now. 'I blamed myself.'

'She shouldn't have done,' said Lizzie.

'But I did,' Vivian responded firmly.

'But – why?' asked Ellie.

'We were rivals – everyone knew that, right?' said Vivian.

'And that rivalry spurred us both on,' added Lizzie. 'It made us both more ambitious.'

'I was determined to catch up with Lizzie, she was determined to stay one step ahead.'

'Between every big competition we were in a race to master new skills,' Lizzie went on. 'We each knew the other would up the difficulty every time. We had to keep up the pace.'

Ellie glanced from one to the other. They seemed so comfortable together – they were almost completing each other's sentences. It was so different from the rivalry she had always imagined.

'Vivian mastered the Produnova vault,' Lizzie was explaining. 'You've probably heard of it. The most prodigiously difficult vault ever performed.'

'Yes – it carries a really high difficulty value,' said Ellie.

'Right,' said Vivian. Ellie remembered how she had reacted when Scarlett had asked if they could learn the Produnova. She saw the same tension in her face now as she spoke. 'That's why I went for it. I was always a power gymnast and vault was the only apparatus where I could pull ahead of Lizzie. With the Produnova I stood a chance of beating her.'

'Vivvy tried it first at Worlds but she didn't quite land it,' said Lizzie. 'I knew she wouldn't make the same mistake at the Olympics, so I started working on it too. I was nearly there, landing it maybe fifty per cent of the time in training.'

Vivian shook her head.

'I knew that I wasn't ready to do it in competition, but I went for it against the coach's advice,' Lizzie admitted. 'I wanted that team gold so badly.

'So you performed the Produnova,' said Ellie.

Lizzie nodded. 'Only I misjudged it, landed badly and – well, you know the rest . . .' She tailed off, as though the memory of that career-ending injury still hurt.

'It was my fault one of the best gymnasts of all time had to retire in her prime,' said Vivian, finishing the story quickly, a quiet intensity in her low voice.

'And that's why you wanted me to be more careful,' Ellie said, as it all started to come together. 'It was because of Lizzie.'

Vivian nodded. 'You remind me of Lizzie so much – not just the way you look – but as a gymnast too. You are capable of great things, but you mustn't be in too much of a rush.'

Ellie blushed at the words 'capable of great things'. They were so unfamiliar coming from Vivian's lips.

'So that's why you sent me to Cornwall.'

'Rowing is the best way in the world to build up the upper body strength you need to develop new vault skills – *safely*!' Vivian looked at her seriously.

'But it wasn't just that. It worried me, Ellie, that you wanted it so much you had hidden an injury.'

'A gymnast needs to be focused, but if that focus becomes unhealthy it's not good for her – or for her gymnastics,' said Lizzie.

'You needed a break,' Vivian said. 'A reminder that there is life beyond the vault, bars, beam and floor!'

'Right,' said Ellie, though she wasn't sure she agreed. She understood that the rowing had helped her vaulting. But as for discovering a world beyond gym – well, the break had just reminded her how empty her world was without it. 'So, what now?'

'Now we get back to work,' said Vivian. 'If you wanna make the Euros squad, you're gonna have to seriously impress this weekend.'

'Do you – do you think I stand a chance?' Ellie murmured quietly.

'Why do you think I've been so tough on you?' asked Vivian. 'You've got potential.'

Ellie flushed hotly, confused but happy.

'But you'll get no special favours from me,' Vivian

insisted. 'I don't care who your aunt is. If you're good enough, you go, but if you're not ready . . .'

'I understand,' said Ellie, who still couldn't get over how lucky she was even to be here. Then she glanced shyly at Lizzie. 'Are you – are you hoping to come to Euros?'

Lizzie shook her head regretfully. 'No. I'm focusing on getting back to full fitness for the Olympics next year.'

She had shifted position so that her right leg was stretched out in front of her. For the first time, Ellie caught sight of the scar running down her calf, a vivid zigzag that told the story of more than ten years of injury, of a time when she'd thought she had lost gym forever. Compared to what Lizzie had been through, Ellie's ankle had been nothing. And if Lizzie could make a comeback, then so could Ellie.

'But you're going to stay here?' asked Ellie. Now that she had finally found her aunt, she wanted to get to know her.

'Yes, and I figured I might help my niece with her

training, too!' said Lizzie. 'That's if you don't mind?'

Ellie broke into a grin. 'Mind? No! It would be everything I've ever dreamed of.'

CHAPTER
Twenty-Five

That day's training session was the best ever. Not only was she back training with the National squad, but Lizzie was there too. As she warmed up, Ellie kept having to glance over at her to check she wasn't dreaming. All of the other Junior squad girls were staring too, but Lizzie didn't act like a big star. She kept her head down and focused on her stretching like she was just another gymnast – although of course she wasn't.

Lizzie was out of practice and her right leg was still weaker than her left. Certain skills were difficult for her. But she hadn't lost the 'thing' that made every one of her moves exquisite to watch. It was hard to put your finger on it – perhaps it was grace, perhaps star quality – from her long, slender expressive fingers, to the lines she made with her arms, the turn of her neck and the expression in her large, velvety dark eyes as she worked . . . There was no doubt about it, Lizzie Trengilly was a gymnast like no other.

'She is blowing my mind away!' said Katya, as the girls crowded round the lockers between rotations for a drink.

'I really don't get why everyone's always going on about the family resemblance,' said Scarlett. Ellie was reminded of all the times people had said she was like her aunt. She'd never realised till now just what a compliment that was. But Scarlett's words also made her remember that this weekend was a competition. There were eleven Junior girls for only five Euros places. They were all rivals now.

At the end of the warm-up, Vivian stood in front of the Junior squad. 'OK, listen up, ladies!' she barked, back to her usual brash self. 'In Berlin we will be up against the best Junior gymnasts in Europe. The Italian team are incredibly strong. Esme Mattari won the Youth Olympics last year, against fierce competition from the Americans.'

'She is tall as beanpole,' whispered Katya. 'And super good on floor and beam!'

'The Germans are also seriously good,' Vivian went on. 'They've got the twins, Georgia and Gaia Kopfler.'

'The double threat!' whispered Bella.

'Not forgetting the Romanians and the Czechs, who always field strong teams. Going up against any of them is going to be a tall order.'

The girls all listened intently.

'We can only take five of you to Berlin,' said Vivian, 'plus one reserve. Which means that some of you are going to be disappointed.'

Ellie felt her stomach contract.

'Remember – gym is all about timing. You may not be ready for Euros now. You might come into your peak in time for the Olympics next year – or you might not.'

Ellie felt sure Vivian was talking to her.

'So give it your all this weekend,' Vivian went on. 'The emphasis for today is floor and beam, tomorrow we'll focus more on vault and bars. Don't walk away thinking you could have done more – leave it all in the gym.'

Ellie quietly looked at her Academy squad mates – Bella, Katya and Scarlett. They were against each other now. Gymnastics had always been about the team for Ellie, and it felt particularly awful to think that some of her best friends were now her competition. The atmosphere was different this weekend. More competitive, with the gymnasts jealously watching each other's performances, no time for camaraderie as each focused on her own goals.

Ellie glanced over to where Tam was working on the rings. He was competing for a place in the boys' squad this weekend – at least he wasn't Ellie's rival. He dismounted and gave her a cheeky wink. Then Ellie caught sight of Lizzie, who smiled at her as well. Yes, she thought, this weekend was going to be hard, but knowing she had Lizzie and Tam on her side felt amazing.

Ellie had three days to prove she was ready for Euros and, thanks to Vivian's crazy Cornish training regime, she wasn't out of the running. It wasn't just the rowing that had helped. Being forced to focus on non-impact skills had sharpened up Ellie's balance – especially on one leg! Her spins and arabesques were now the best they'd ever been. She'd even worked a new skill into her beam routine – her bad leg lifted vertically to her nose and held there whilst she spun, not once but twice, without a wobble.

'Well, it looks like having one leg out of action has had its benefits!' Barbara Steele commented as she watched Ellie at work. Ellie flushed and nearly fell off the beam with happiness.

Vivian was less complimentary. She was walking round with a clipboard, noting every single mistake each gymnast made. And Ellie came in for her fair share of criticism. 'Stick your bum in on that spin, Trengilly,' she barked. 'You look like a stork on the toilet!'

Vivian might have let Ellie in on her Lizzie

secret but that didn't seem to mean that she was going to let up on her in training.

'You've got to punch the floor on landing, Trengilly . . . your arm's so bendy it looks like a jelly snake . . . is that a sheep jump? It looks more like a lamb chop, Trengilly . . .' But each time she yelled 'Trengilly' both Ellie and Lizzie would look up, so in the end she took to calling Ellie 'Little Trengilly', or 'Little T', and somehow that took the sting out of even her worst comments.

'Plant that landing or you won't stick it, Little T,' she yelled. 'No – more oomph!'

Ellie smiled. She knew now that Vivian was being hard on her because she thought she had potential.

In fact, the only thing seriously spoiling Ellie's joy at being back in the gym was her ankle. The doctor had told her that 'crystal foot syndrome' could last for some time, but no matter how often she tried to reassure herself that it was all a figment of her imagination, she couldn't throw off a nagging sense of anxiety every time she landed on it. They were training on competition surfaces now and Ellie found that she was holding back on her landings and dismounts, fearful of hurting herself again. But her ankle bore up well. She expected to be in agony by the end of the first day, but there was nothing more than a dull throb – scarcely more than the ache she felt all over.

'How's the crock ankle doing, then?' asked Vivian, seeing Ellie holding her foot in her hand as she sat by the lockers at the end of the session. 'Tell it to me straight.'

'It's OK,' said Ellie, who was determined to be totally honest now. 'I just don't quite . . . I don't know . . . I don't trust it any more.'

Vivian knelt and took Ellie's foot in her hand, rotating and inspecting it. 'No swelling,' she said. 'That's good. I still want you to get some ice on it and show it to Sam, though. No point taking any risks.'

Ellie didn't argue this time. Maybe seeing Sam would put her mind at rest. She made her way over to the medical room and Sam greeted her cheerfully.

'Good to see you back, missus!' he said. 'And

looking in good shape too, may I say!'

'Thanks,' she said. 'I feel good.'

'Vivvy's no fool!' Sam said, after he checked her over. 'I thought there'd be some stiffness from the boot, but my guess is that you're in better shape now than you were before you left.'

Ellie smiled. 'That's the rowing, I guess.'

'And she had you doing kinaesthetic stuff too, right?'

Ellie looked puzzled.

'Tiny movements – rotating a ball with your toes, that kind of thing.'

'Oh, yes, she did,' said Ellie. 'I wondered what that was for.'

'It's even more important than the muscle stuff,' Sam explained. 'Think about it – on bar or beam, a millimetre is the difference between sticking a landing and wiping out, so you need to be in control of the tiniest movements.'

'So all those funny exercises had a point to them, after all?'

'They certainly did.'

'And are there . . .' Ellie hesitated. 'Are there exercises for my brain – to make me trust my foot again?'

Sam looked sympathetic. 'Learning to trust your body again will take time.'

Ellie nodded. She just didn't know if it was time she had.

As she made her way to the dining hall, where the others had all gone for supper, she nearly tripped over Memory Danster. The girl was sitting on her own on the steps outside the gym, eating a sandwich.

'Oh – um – hi,' said Ellie. She hadn't spoken to Memory since she'd come back, although that wasn't exactly new. Memory hardly seemed to talk to anyone except the coaches. 'I'm just going to the dining hall – if you want to come too?' she asked.

Memory shook her head. 'No.' Then after a second she added a gruff, 'Thanks.'

'Oh – right,' said Ellie, turning away and feeling

troubled. It didn't feel right, leaving Memory on her own like that. But then she remembered all the millions of questions she wanted to ask Lizzie. All thoughts of Memory were forgotten as Ellie hurried off to the dining hall to find her aunt.

CHAPTER
Twenty-Six

'What was it like winning World Championships?'

'How did it feel being the best GB gymnast of all time?'

'When did you start training again?'

In the dining hall, half of the Junior squad were all clustered around Lizzie, firing questions at the famous gymnast.

'How did you feel when you found out you were cured?' Bella asked with shining eyes.

'I still don't know for sure,' said Lizzie, with the smile that Ellie had seen on so many podium photos. 'I've no idea if I'll be able to get back to the level I was at my peak.'

'But you're going to try?' asked Eva Reddle dreamily. 'I think that's so wonderful!'

Lizzie nodded. 'I have to give it a go or I'll regret it for the rest of my life.'

All of the younger gymnasts nodded. They understood – they shared Lizzie's dream. They wouldn't be here if they didn't.

'And why you not tell everyone you are training again?' asked Katya.

'I was afraid,' Lizzie admitted. 'Afraid I might not be able to do it. That I might have to quit all over again. I wasn't sure I could do that with the world watching.'

Ellie could hardly imagine the great Lizzie Trengilly being afraid of anything.

'I guess now the secret's out it'll be big news,' said Tam. 'Trengilly back in training!'

Lizzie laughed. 'I suppose it might be,' she said with a shrug. 'It's an added pressure but one I suppose I'm ready for now.'

'So who actually knew you were here?' asked Ellie.

'Emma knew – and Fran – and your dad – I couldn't exactly keep my big brother out of the loop,' she smiled. 'And Barbara and, of course, Viv.'

Scarlett smirked at Ellie, who couldn't help feeling a slight sting of hurt pride. She knew what Scarlett was thinking: why hadn't Lizzie trusted her too?

'I still don't get why you told Vivian,' said Tam.

'Vivian was the one who read about the experimental surgery,' said Lizzie. 'She got in touch with the surgeon, sent him all my details and persuaded him to take on my case. I owe all this to her.'

'Wow!' said Scarlett. She might resent Ellie's connection with Lizzie, but even she couldn't resist the magic of her story. 'She did all that for someone who was her rival, who beat her every single time?'

Tam laughed. 'I guess that idea might be hard for *you* to understand, Scarlett!'

'I just think it's the most exciting story ever,' said Bella. 'Old rivals, now the best of friends. I hope the newspapers write all about that too!'

'And it'll have the happiest ending when you

win that Olympic medal,' said Eva.

Lizzie laughed. 'It's a long road to the Olympics and a lot can happen in a year. Anyway,' she went on, turning the focus away from herself, 'right now it's about you girls going to Berlin for Euros!'

'My parents have already booked into the most expensive hotel in the city,' said Scarlett, looking very pleased with herself.

'Wow,' said Bella, her eyebrows shooting up sky-high. 'They must be pretty confident you'll make the squad.'

Scarlett shrugged like the idea of her not making the squad wasn't even a possibility. 'I can't wait to see them. They've been away on business, but Mummy said she wouldn't miss Euros for anything. And our hotel is five star!'

'Well, I'd be happy to stay in a cardboard box if I could just get a place on the squad!' said Ellie.

'Me too!' said Bella.

Ellie shivered – but she wasn't sure if it was with fear or hope. She'd given up believing Euros were even a possibility. Now the possibility was back on the table she felt more terrified than ever – the hope was almost worse than the despair. It was like Lizzie said – thinking she'd lost out once was bad enough. She wasn't sure she could bear to lose her dream again.

After the others had gone, Ellie and Lizzie wandered to Ellie's room and sat on the balcony gazing out over the moon-soaked lawns.

'I'm sorry I kept you in the dark,' said Lizzie. 'Your dad and I figured you had so much of your own trouble going on, you didn't need to worry about keeping my secret too.'

'I understand,' said Ellie, and – finally – she did. All her feelings of jealousy and hurt seemed to melt away as she realised that Lizzie had just been trying to protect her. 'Although it's weird to think you were here all along.'

'Apparently you nearly bumped into me during one of your 'secret' training sessions!' laughed Lizzie. 'Yes – Tam confessed to what the two of you have been up to! He was worried it was all his fault you'd been injured.'

'Oh no!' Ellie's stomach clenched tightly. 'I mean – it wasn't his idea. Did I get him in trouble?'

'He got a formal warning,' said Lizzie. 'You only escaped one because Barbara thinks your injury was punishment enough! But you *both* need to keep out of mischief from now on!'

Ellie felt guilty but relieved. At least Tam hadn't been thrown out of the GB squad because of her.

Lizzie grinned mischievously and added, 'He seems like a nice boy!'

Ellie flushed hotly. 'He's not . . . that is – I mean . . . we're just good friends!'

'Did I suggest anything else?' said Lizzie, still with a twinkle in her eye.

Ellie changed the subject quickly. 'So *that's* how Vivian found out what we were up to!'

'Afraid so!' said Lizzie.

Ellie sighed. 'If I'd been able to ask you about Vivian, I'd have known she was on my side. Then maybe I wouldn't have been so stupid.'

'Vivian is a complicated woman,' said Lizzie. 'I can see she's tough on you, but that's because she rates you. And her training methods are unusual, but she knows what she's doing. You wouldn't believe the things she'd had me doing – but it's all worked. You have to trust her.'

'I do,' said Ellie. And to her surprise, she realised she meant it.

CHAPTER
Twenty-Seven

'How was the big race?' Ellie asked over Skype that evening.

'We smashed it!' said Nancy, beaming out from the computer screen. 'Third place. Only beaten by the Roseland Posse and that crew from the Isles of Scilly who win practically every year – and Lucy was epic.'

Lucy flushed happily. '*And* Nancy and the rest of the crew got a special heroes' salute thing for their bravery last week,' she said. 'The lifeboat did a fly-by – only on the water, not in the air, obviously – and the local press took pictures of us and everything.'

'It was pretty epic,' added Nancy. 'Why you'd want to miss it to get back into a stuffy gym beats me!'

'Because tomorrow they'll announce the squad for Euros,' said Tam, who was leaning over Ellie's shoulder to chat to his ruddy-faced sister.

'Stop stressing, bro,' said Nancy. 'You're a dead cert for the boys' squad!'

Tam shrugged. 'Nothing is certain in gymnastics.'

'OK, but unless you get carried off by aliens, or trampled by a rhinoceros – which would be kind of cool – you'll ace it!' grinned Nancy.

Tam just shrugged. He might be Junior British Champ, but he was taking nothing for granted.

'What about the girls' squad?' asked Lucy. 'Who do you reckon they'll go for?'

'Memory's the strongest all-around performer,' said Ellie. 'Then Eva Reddle.'

'Bella looked amazing too,' said Katya, hugging Bella so tightly she made her blush.

'Oh – and Scarlett's so certain she'll make it that her parents have already booked front-row seats,' added Tam.

'Seriously?' laughed Nancy.

'Yup! Which leaves one place, plus a reserve,' said Ellie.

'I know it won't be me,' said Katya with a little shrug. 'It is only my first year as Junior and there are still many mistakes in my gymnastics.'

'But your floor and beam are exquisite,' said Ellie.

Katya shrugged. 'No – it will be Ellie! She can do things on bar that even Seniors are not able to do.'

'But there are still questions about my fitness,' said Ellie, flushing nervously. '*And* we've got vault tomorrow.'

She hadn't even admitted to herself until that moment how nervous she was about getting back on the vault again. Even the thought of a single Yurchenko on a competition surface made her wince – and she knew that she needed to be strong on every single piece of apparatus to earn a spot on the squad. She couldn't afford to hold back – and yet part of her was so frightened of going for it. She needed to overcome that, and fast.

CHAPTER
Twenty-Eight

Ellie dreamed of the vault that night – only, in her dream, she was Lizzie. She was at the Olympics, watching Vivian perform a perfect Produnova. Then it was her turn. She stood at the start of the runway, and stared at the vault looming up in front of her. She felt a thrill of fear that chilled her to ice. Then she was running, hitting the board, in the air, twisting, arching, landing . . . screaming, clutching her foot, seeing it shatter, watching her career breaking into a thousand tiny pieces on the vault corridor.

She woke in a cold sweat in the morning light

and couldn't get back to sleep after that.

'Did you hear Memory's got a perfect Amanar?' Phoebe was saying as the girls lined up by the vault to show off their skills to the selectors. 'She's been working on it since squad camp and now it's competition ready.'

'Which will make her unbeatable,' said Niamh, biting her nails anxiously. 'She must know she's guaranteed a spot on the squad now.'

Ellie could sense the same tension that she was feeling in the other girls. They were all competing against each other for those five coveted spots, and that made it incredibly tense between them.

'She doesn't look very happy about it though, does she?' said Eva, glancing over to the vault where Memory stood looking straight ahead, stony-faced.

'I keep trying to talk to her,' said Bella. 'I asked her about training in America and everything. But she just changes the subject or walks away.'

'Sometimes she acts like she doesn't even want to be here at all,' said Katya.

Ellie watched Memory perform a perfect Amanar

and then dismount with military precision. She was certainly a mystery.

'That was fantastic,' Ellie said when Memory walked back up the runway, but Memory ignored her. She was staring out of the window where the leaves of a great oak tree were fluttering against the glass, the sun glinting through them and casting dappled patterns of light and shade on to the vault corridor.

Ellie sighed. She had tried. And she needed to concentrate on her own performance now, anyway.

Scarlett was up next, with a flawless double Yurchenko.

'See what some of us have been up to whilst you've been sunning yourself by the seaside,' Scarlett said as she made her way back after the vault.

'Just ignore her,' whispered Bella. 'She gets worse when she's nervous.'

'What is she nervous about?'

'Despite all her showing off, she's worried she might not make the squad,' said Bella. 'Especially now you're back.'

Ellie glanced at Scarlett, who was chalking her hands up furiously. She'd got so used to Scarlett being unpleasant that she'd never asked why she was acting that way. Could all her nastiness really just be because she was nervous?

But now Vivian was calling her name.

'You ready to show us what your time in the boat has taught you, Little Trengilly?' she asked.

Ellie stepped up to the runway. She looked at the stretch of mats in front of her, at the red felt top of the vault and the safety mat beyond it. Her stomach contracted at the thought of the landing. She nodded.

'Good. I want you to try an Amanar.'

Ellie looked up in astonishment. 'Seriously?

Vivian shrugged. 'Unless you don't want to?'

'I do – but – you said . . .'

'I said you weren't strong enough then, and you weren't,' said Vivian. 'But Langer's training has built you up. I'd like to see you try the more difficult vault.'

'But she's been out of training for over a month!'

219

protested Scarlett, her face pink with indignation.

'No, Miss Atkins, she has been on a *special* training programme for a month – one designed to develop her strength and expand her repertoire as a gymnast.' Vivian turned back to Ellie. 'So, let's give it a go,' she said. 'I know you've got the technique. Let's see what my old mate Langer has done for those puny muscles of yours.'

It was Ellie's turn to flush now. She stared ahead at the runway. It was hard not think of the other girls watching her, of her foot, of what had happened last time she'd vaulted here – and of what had happened to Lizzie at the Olympics . . .

She hesitated, then took a deep breath and hurtled into the run up. Everything went in slow motion as she ran. The vault suddenly looked bigger than ever before, the landing strip miles beyond. She hurtled at full speed towards the springboard and then . . . she stopped.

Like a horse pulling up before a fence, she shied away from the vault. She'd spooked.

'Don't waste my time, Little Trengilly,' Vivian

said. 'Come on – try again.'

Ellie was aware of other adults watching now. Barbara Steele had wandered over, and so had Lizzie. She went over to chalk up again, her face aflame.

'Can you imagine if she did that at Euros?' she could hear Scarlett saying. 'Seriously – she needs to get a grip!'

Ellie's head was hammering. She knew how much was resting on this.

'You can do it,' said a quiet voice next to her.

Ellie turned to see Memory Danster working on pull-ups on the wall bars. The girl's voice was low and she barely looked Ellie in the eye as she spoke.

'I guess I'm just frightened,' Ellie admitted.

'What is there to be frightened of?' Memory said, an odd expression on her face. 'There are worse things than face-planting on the vault, you know.'

Ellie flushed. Memory was right, of course. She smiled and started to say thanks, but Memory had already turned away.

Ellie took the run up again, and this time she didn't spook. She recalled all the things Vivian had told her in training – and she channelled something else, too. She knew she had new strength in her shoulders from the gig rowing, and that she'd faced fears far worse than this when they'd gone into the inlet to save the kayakers. She soared into the vault, willed her body into the double and found it responding easily. She twisted once, twice, into the Amanar and then rotated easily towards the floor.

But at the last moment she held something back. She didn't commit to the landing, hesitated and stumbled back on to her bum.

'Not bad,' said Vivian. 'Shame about the landing.'

Suddenly, Ellie felt even worse than she had before. She'd done the difficult bit but she'd still flunked it. She'd stalled at the last minute. If she couldn't overcome her fear of the landing, she'd be no use on the Euros squad at all.

'I think – maybe I should just work on double Yurchenkos for a bit.'

'Nope,' said Vivian. 'You're going for the Amanar. Now do it again – and again – until it's perfect.'

CHAPTER
Twenty-Nine

All day the gymnasts worked their socks off. The atmosphere had changed since the last squad camp. There was a new intensity, a crackling sense of ambition, fear and competitiveness now that they were fighting as individuals for those coveted Euros squad places. Scarlett became more unfriendly, Memory was quieter and more withdrawn, Katya was giddy with nerves and Bella walked around like a pale ghost. Even Eva Reddle had taken to chewing her hair, though Ellie couldn't imagine what she had to worry about.

Ellie worked so hard that it seemed like she was

eating, sleeping and breathing gymnastics. She felt strong and confident in everything except the vault, where she continued to work on the Amanar without success. In fact, she was sure her landing was getting worse and worse. She knew the problem was just in her head, but she couldn't shake off the niggling fear that prevented her from planting her landing with the force she needed. By the end of the day there was no more she could do.

It was lovely having Lizzie around. She felt like a big sister rather than an aunt.

'You've put your heart and soul into it,' said Lizzie, putting an arm around Ellie as they made their way over to where Barbara Steele was waiting to announce the Euros selections results. 'You've done all you can.'

'That's just it,' said Ellie with a sigh. 'I don't feel I have.' She hesitated, wanting to explain to Lizzie but not sure how. 'It was like something was holding me back on the vault and I wasn't strong enough to fight it.'

'Sometimes getting mentally ready to compete is

harder than physical readiness,' said Lizzie. 'For a long time after the surgery I was too scared to go near the gym.'

'Really?'

'Yup! Vivian practically had to bully me into it,' smiled Lizzie. 'Sometimes you just need something or someone to help you break free of the things that are holding you back.'

Lizzie squeezed Ellie tight, and Ellie suddenly realised that she desperately wanted a Euros spot, not just for herself, but to make Lizzie proud.

Barbara lined up the whole squad on the practice floor, and she and Vivian stood to address them.

'OK, girls, this is it!' she said with a smile. She was a tiny, elegant lady – she looked more like a former ballerina than a world-class athlete who had competed against Comaneci and the Russian greats. 'You have all done brilliantly, and I would be proud to take any one of you along to Euros. Unfortunately, I can only take five.'

Ellie felt Katya slip her fingers through hers. On the other side, she reached out for Bella's hand. Despite the tension of the weekend, the three Academy gymnasts stood together now, awaiting their fate.

'So without further ado, here are the five gymnasts who will be competing in Berlin.' Barbara paused for just a second and Ellie found she was struggling to breathe.

'Memory Danster.'

Memory stepped forwards. Her face was a mask, not giving away any emotion at the decision.

'Eva Reddle!'

Eva gave a little shriek and made her way to the floor, blushing happily.

'Bella Chee.'

Bella squeezed Ellie's hand and gave the tiniest of sobs. Ellie hugged her. 'You deserve it so much!' she whispered in her ear, and she really meant it. Bella had worked quietly and intensely for years, never making a fuss, never pushing herself forwards, just intently striving for personal perfection. Ellie was thrilled for her.

But her heart was pounding now. Just two spots left on the squad.

'Scarlett Atkins.'

Scarlett punched the air. For a second Ellie thought she saw a look of relief cross the gymnast's face but then she made her way up to the front with a satisfied smirk.

Just one spot left. Ellie looked around at the other girls – Phoebe, Willow, Katya, Niamh, Rosa. They were all amazing gymnasts. Any one of them would deserve a spot on the squad. There was no way it would be her. This wasn't her time – she just knew it.

She was so busy telling herself that she would work towards the Olympics and not let this setback bother her that she wasn't even aware Barbara had called the last name until she realised that Katya was nudging her.

'It's you! It's you!'

'What?'

Ellie looked up and saw that everyone was looking at her. Barbara Steele laughed and said, 'Sorry to interrupt, Miss Trengilly, but I think you've just been selected for Euros!'

She'd been so busy daydreaming that she hadn't noticed that her dream was coming true. In a daze, she started to step forwards, then stopped and turned to hug Katya. She felt awful about letting her little squad mate go.

And then, all of a sudden, she didn't have to.

'Reserve – Katya Popolova,' Barbara was saying.

Katya squeaked like she'd been shot and jumped about six feet in the air, nearly knocking Ellie over. 'Me! Me! Me!' She bounced like a little sprite across the floor and dragged Ellie and Bella into the biggest hug ever. Ellie burst into floods of tears – tears of relief and joy and happiness for her friends and for herself.

Afterwards, Katya kept saying, 'Why are you crying, Ellie? Is *good* news, yes!'

'Yes! Yes!' sobbed Ellie, laughing through her tears. 'It's just – it's all so unbelievable. After everything that has happened, I never thought . . .'

'It takes nearly losing something to make you realise how much you want it, right?' said a voice from behind her.

Ellie turned to see Lizzie, who was beaming from ear to ear. 'I'm so proud of you!'

'I think it was you being there that did it!' said Ellie.

'No way!' said Lizzie. 'You were looking pretty supercharged all by yourself, Little T!'

Ellie looked around at the others. Bella and Katya were dancing round excitedly, being congratulated by Niamh and Phoebe. Eva was comforting her squad mate Willow, who was wiping away tears, reminding Ellie that for every happy ending there was someone else whose dream had come crashing down around their shoulders. Then there was Scarlett, already texting her family. And Memory, packing up her kit bag, ready to go back to her room.

'I'm going to Euros!' said Ellie in an awed whisper. 'Can you believe it? I'm going to Euros!'

CHAPTER
Thirty

The next week was a whirlwind. Now they were down to just six in the squad, training was more intense than ever. And if Ellie had thought Vivian was tough on them before, it was nothing compared to how she was now that Euros were in sight. Every single move had to be perfected, polished, fine-tuned. Ellie was so focused on honing her vault to perfection that she started doing it in her sleep – but she still couldn't land the Amanar, either waking or sleeping.

And there was everything else that needed to be done before they headed to Germany – passports and tickets, medicals and kitting out the squad, as well as press interviews and photoshoots. This side of things was totally new to Ellie, and completely bewildering too. There was a flurry of interest in the Junior GB Euros squad from gymnastics magazines, local newspapers and even the national press.

'There was a bit about you and Tam on *Cornwall Tonight!*' Lucy told her excitedly when she called home one day.

No one except Tam himself had been surprised that he'd been appointed captain of the boys' Junior Euros squad. Nancy, in particular, was bursting with pride – although Ellie knew there was no way she was going to tell Tam that.

'There was a fab pic of Ellie in the *Falmouth Packet!*' said Nancy. 'Tam nearly cracked the camera, of course.'

'Well, they do say twins look alike!' Tam retorted quickly.

It was amazing and exciting and horribly nerve-wracking all at once. Ellie was thrilled to be sharing the whole experience with Bella and Katya, and it was awesome that Tam was coming along too. Her only twinge of sadness was that the Junior squad didn't really feel connected. They weren't competing against each other in training any more, but things still felt strained. There was no sense of the team spirit that Ellie had felt when she was competing with her Academy squad. Eva was lovely, of course, but Memory was still acting as if the others barely existed, and Scarlett, who had never exactly been a team player, was worse than ever.

'She's acting like she's European Champion already!' Ellie told Nancy.

'I bet she's just loving the photoshoots!' Nancy laughed.

'She is pouting like a fish and thinking she is a supermodel,' said Katya, doing an impression of Scarlett posing for the cameras that had the others in stitches.

'At least *she* smiles,' said Tam. 'Memory just frowns, like going to Euros is the worst thing that's ever happened to her.'

'Tam's right,' said Ellie. 'One of the interviewers

started asking her about training in America the other day and she just cut them dead.' She sighed. 'I can't work that girl out.'

'Lucky you've got Eva as captain,' said Nancy. 'She's a sweetie.'

'And we'll be there too!' squeaked Lucy excitedly. 'I can't believe Aunt Lizzie managed to swing tickets for all of us – and flights and hotels too. I don't know how she did it.'

'Mum says that people in the gymnastics world will do anything for Lizzie,' said Nancy. 'Because she's such a massive star.'

Ellie had thought she knew what a celebrity Lizzie Trengilly was, but she was realising that she had no idea! The news of Lizzie's remarkable recovery and return to the gym had gone viral. It even featured on the front pages of several national newspapers. When the GB squad arrived at the airport to fly to Berlin, they were swamped by reporters, all wanting to take pictures and get an interview.

'Is it true you're back in training, Lizzie?'

'Yes, it's true.'

'And you're going to be back for the Olympics?'

'I hope so,' said Lizzie with a shy smile. 'But who knows.'

'Did we hear you have your old rival to thank for your recovery?'

'Yes, I do,' said Lizzie, putting her arms around Vivian, who was standing next to her.

Vivian just rolled her eyes. 'I don't know what I was thinking!'

All the cameras clicked, wanting to get pictures of the two women together.

'Do you wish you were competing in Berlin, Lizzie?'

'I'd love to be competing, but I'm not ready yet,' she said. 'Right now you should be looking at the new generation of stars – Sian Edwards and Sophia Mitford in the Seniors squad, and the Juniors, who are all looking incredibly strong.'

'Including your niece. Is that right, Lizzie? Is there a new Trengilly in waiting? Is she as good as you?'

Lizzie turned to Ellie and smiled. 'It's her first time in a big competition,' said Lizzie. 'And she's just back from injury . . .'

'Like you . . .'

'Like me!'

'Is that all you have in common?'

'Why don't you wait and let Ellie prove what she can do,' said Lizzie. 'Obviously I think she's a wonderful gymnast – but I may be a little biased!'

Lizzie winked at Ellie and she smiled back, grateful to her aunt for not building her up too much. She already felt pressure to live up to her name, and now she found herself mentioned in every article about Lizzie. Everyone was asking the same question: 'Will Ellie Trengilly be as good as her talented aunt?'

'I don't see why Ellie is getting all the attention,' said Scarlett crossly as they made their way from the airport in Berlin straight to the arena. They were heading there for podium training before they even checked into the hotel.

'And I don't see why you even care,' snapped Memory.

'Hey! Press – photographs – interviews – that's just a sideshow,' Vivian reminded them sharply. 'You girls are here to perform, remember!'

Ellie didn't think she could possibly forget it. It was all she ever thought about at the moment. As they made their way into the arena, Ellie felt a flutter of nerves and excitement. Podium training helped gymnasts get used to the space they would be competing in, the spring of the floor, the layout of the apparatus. It also gave them a chance to suss out the other competitors, and Ellie caught her first sight of the Italian team working out on the floors. Her gaze was drawn to Esme Mattari. The Olympic Youth Champion was slender, tall for a gymnast and very beautiful. Her white-blonde hair made Scarlett's look brassy and cheap in comparison.

'She doesn't exactly look Italian, though, does she?' asked Bella. 'More like a Scandinavian goddess.'

Esme's teammates were equally glamorous, even in their practice leos, and the German team looked incredibly strong too. Gaia and Georgia Kopfler were twin sisters whom the gym press were tipping as the 'double threat'. They were on home soil, too, and the crowd would be behind them, which was a huge advantage.

Ellie remembered Emma once saying that some teams used podium training to freak out the opposition, and the Germans were doing just that – throwing incredible tumbles and complex skills on every piece of apparatus. The Italian team were keeping something back, though, not showing off their best moves – as if they didn't even need to. Ellie couldn't figure out which was most intimidating.

'So, the team competition is tomorrow,' Vivian reminded them as they warmed up. 'But the top individual scores qualify for individual all-around and apparatus finals.'

They all nodded.

'But that doesn't mean you're just to look out for yourself,' Vivian went on, glancing at Scarlett as she spoke. 'You need to be a team. You should support each other, have each other's backs. You can lift everyone's game if you work together.'

Ellie glanced at the others. She knew she, Eva, Katya and Bella were team players. But Scarlett and Memory?

'That's why I've booked a team dorm for you all to

stay in at the hotel,' said Vivian. 'You'll be spending every waking minute together as a team for the next few days – and every sleeping minute, too.'

'But . . .' Memory started to object, but Scarlett got there first.

'I'm staying with my parents. In the best hotel in town. They've booked the penthouse suite.'

Vivian rolled her eyes. 'And is there room for the rest of the squad in this swanky penthouse of yours?'

'Of course not,' said Scarlett sniffily. 'It's very exclusive.'

'Then I'm afraid you're staying with the squad – at least until the competition's over.'

'But my parents are dying to see me,' whined Scarlett. 'I haven't seen them since Christmas!'

'And they can see you in the arena tomorrow, like all of the other families!' said Vivian firmly.

Scarlett gave an angry 'hmmph!' and Katya sighed. Ellie knew that her parents hadn't been able to get away from the circus. Not that Scarlett seemed to notice.

'It's so unfair!' she said crossly.

'Oh, just shut up!'

They all turned in surprise. Memory's eyes flashed dangerously. 'Can't you just shut up for a single minute?'

Then she stormed off, leaving the rest of the squad staring after her.

'What's up with her?' asked Scarlett. 'So much for team bonding. Did you hear how she spoke to me?'

'Memory's got a lot on her mind,' said Vivian with an anxious frown.

'What do you mean?' asked Ellie.

'Just don't be too hard on her. She's trying her best.'

'Well I'd hate to see her at her worst, then!' said Scarlett. 'Come on. Let's get to this stupid hotel – although if any of you snore, I'm going to check myself out right away!'

That evening the GB squads, Senior and Junior, boys' and girls', had a team meal together before being sent off for an early night. Scarlett sat with a scowl on her face the whole time. The other Junior girls all felt a bit flat too. Maybe it was nerves, or Scarlett's contagious bad mood, but even Tam's constant stream of jokes failed to keep up their spirits. The usually cheerful Eva complained of feeling under the weather as they were all climbing into bed later.

'You look really pale,' said Bella, who was looking more childlike than ever in a cotton nightdress covered with teddy bears.

'I've got a bit of a headache,' said Eva. 'Probably just nerves.'

'I hope you are not getting sick!' said Katya anxiously. 'You are our best gymnast.'

'Oh, well, that's nice!' said Scarlett. She was wearing a pair of pink silk pyjamas, her hair lying in a sheet of gold over her shoulders. 'I think you'll find I'm just as good as she is.'

'Never mind who's the best gymnast in the squad,' said Ellie. 'We want *everyone* on top form tomorrow. We're a team, remember?'

'It's not *me* who needs reminding,' said Scarlett, glancing significantly over to the bed in the corner where Memory was curled up with her headphones on, acting like none of the others existed.

Ellie felt a twinge of sadness. This wasn't how she'd imagined it would be. It was her first international competition – her first time representing GB. She'd thought the squad would feel like a team, all supporting each other and backing one another up. Instead, they were all bickering, and that made her anxious. What effect would those tensions have on the gym floor tomorrow?

'Let's all just concentrate on getting a good night's sleep!' said Bella. 'We have the biggest competition of our lives tomorrow, remember?'

But Ellie was so nervous it took her ages to get to sleep. When she finally did drop off, she dreamed of the arena, of Esme Mattari in her glamorous leotard, of the 'double threat' Kopfler twins tumbling across the floor – and the vault, always the vault, which haunted her dreams all night long.

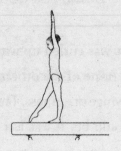

CHAPTER
Thirty-One

The next morning, as they made their way over to the arena, Eva was looking paler than ever.

'I just feel a bit woolly,' she explained. 'I haven't woken up properly yet. But I'll be fine once I start competing.'

'You'd better be!' said Scarlett unsympathetically. 'I don't want to miss out on a medal just because you have a sore head.'

Ellie sighed. Scarlett clearly hadn't discovered her team spirit overnight!

The event was a sell-out. Every single seat in the arena was full, with gym fans thronging to the competition from all over Europe. There was a great atmosphere, too. Giant flags draped over the railings and the crowds of supporters were dressed in their national colours with team slogans painted on their cheeks. Banners bore the names of individual gymnasts, and whole families wore t-shirts with photos of their favourite competitor.

Ellie was glad she'd faced a big arena at British Champs earlier in the year, but it still was hard not to feel a bit overawed by the scale of the event. During the warm-up she glanced up at the crowd and reminded herself that Nancy, Lucy and her parents were out there somewhere, with the twins' mum, Mandy Moffat. She hoped they would be sitting with Eva and Bella's parents too. Scarlett's mum and dad were apparently in 'the expensive seats', though.

'So they get the best view of the winners' podium when I get my medal!' Scarlett explained.

'We have to beat the Italians and the Germans first!' Bella reminded her with a smile.

'Oh, I don't think we stand a chance as a team,'

Scarlett declared airily. 'I'm focusing on my own performance today so I can qualify for individual all-around finals.'

Ellie caught Bella's eye.

'You do remember what Vivian told us, right?' Ellie asked. 'How if we work as a team we can lift each other's performance?'

'Obviously . . .' said Scarlett. 'But Memory has pretty much checked out of the team already and Eva looks like she's about to pass out. I don't exactly rate our chances, do you?'

Scarlett was right. The team event seemed to go wrong from the start, and it didn't help that they were starting on vault. As Ellie stood on the runway, waiting for the signal to begin, a wave of fear washed over her. She lost her nerve in the run up, bottled the Amanar and just went for a one and half Yurchenko. She landed it neatly, but felt mad at herself nonetheless. Her execution score would be good, but she knew her difficulty value would be way lower than it could have been.

Memory nailed her Amanar, but then Eva stumbled forwards and fell on her face as she landed. Ellie had never seen Eva so much as wobble before, and when she looked at the team captain she saw that her face was pale and clammy.

'Are you OK?' she asked.

Eva nodded. 'I'm so sorry – I just – I don't know what happened.'

'Sorry!' Scarlett huffed impatiently. 'You do realise we were counting on a good score from at least one of you two there? It's not like Bella's any good on vault!'

'That is not nice!' said Katya, who was supporting the rest of the team on the competition floor. 'And you is also wobbling when you are landing.'

After that things went from bad to worse. On the bars Scarlett fell off, and Eva missed her Tcatchev and narrowly avoided falling off in her Mo salto.

'I'm sorry,' she said when she dismounted, her usual sunny smile nowhere to be seen. 'I just – I don't seem to be quite on the ball today.'

'Are you sure you're feeling OK?' asked Vivian.

'I'm fine . . . honestly.'

But as she went up for the floor rotation, it was clear that Eva was far from fine. She assumed her starting position and waited for the signal to begin. Ellie thought she saw her sway a little, but then she pulled herself taut.

'Is she OK?' asked Bella, her keen eyes also catching the wobble.

'I don't know,' said Ellie. 'She looks awfully pale.'

Then the music started and Eva stayed completely still.

'What's going on?' said Katya.

'Something's wrong!' said Ellie in alarm.

Eva swayed like a slender tree in the wind. For a moment she seemed to resist gravity, and then she lost the battle and fainted clean away. Everyone rushed around her, but Vivian was there first, calling Sam the doctor to her side.

It seemed like hours later – but was probably only a few seconds – when Eva awoke, her face ashen.

'I'm sorry,' she whispered. 'I just don't think I

can go on.'

'You're not wrong there, kid!' said Vivian.

Ellie's heart was breaking. At that moment she didn't care about the team competition. She just knew how much this meant to Eva!

'Oh that's great!' said Scarlett. 'We're already way behind the Germans and Italians, and now you're going to leave us in the lurch.'

'I'm sorry to let you all down,' whispered Eva.

'You're in no fit state to continue,' said Vivian, glaring at Scarlett. 'I shouldn't have let you perform at all today.'

'What do we do now?' Ellie asked Vivian, who was looking as anxious as she felt.

'I guess we see what our little understudy can pull out of the bag,' she said, turning to Katya, whose eyes went as round as saucers.

'Me?'

'Yup, kiddo,' said Vivian with a smile. 'I'll go speak to the organisers. It's unusual to bring in a substitute mid-competition, but under the circumstances we don't have any choice.'

Sam was helping Eva to her feet. 'This is your chance!' she said to Katya.

'But you is working so hard – your beautiful floor . . .'

'Hey, the crowd are going to love your circus routine!' smiled Eva, only her eyes betraying the sadness she really felt.

It was heartbreaking watching Eva making her way out of the arena, supported by Vivian and Sam. The crowd applauded wildly, but that only made it seem crueller. This could have been Eva's moment – but it had been taken away in the blink of an eye.

With Eva gone, the competition resumed. Scarlett went up on to the floor, messed up her final tumble sequence and came off looking tearful and angry.

'All this stuff with Eva has completely blown my concentration!' she complained.

Ellie bit her tongue and tried to be supportive. 'You've got beam next,' she said. 'And you're Queen of the Beam, remember!'

Scarlett rolled her eyes and didn't even bother to reply.

Memory was powerful in her tumbles, but her performance lacked any conviction. She barely managed a smile. Even Bella wasn't at her best, and they still didn't know if Katya was going to be eligible to perform. Ellie knew she had to step up for the team. She couldn't hold anything back – she had to throw all she had into her floor routine. The piece was a dazzling spectacle, and Ellie performed it today with a sense of urgency and passion drawn from all her recent experiences – the agony of injury, the terror in the inlet, the joy of finding Aunt Lizzie and the pain of Eva's plight. She was amazed when she came to the end and saw the crowd go wild.

'That was beautiful!' said Katya. 'Your spins were electric!'

'And *you'll* be even better!' said Ellie. The organisers had finally agreed to let Katya perform and she was jittery with excitement.

'I am wishing my family was here!' she said.

'Your family *are* here!' said Ellie. 'Your gym

family. Me and Nancy, Bella, Tam – all of us!'

Katya beamed and skipped out on to the floor.

The crowd loved Katya's routine. It was impossible not to – it was circus-inspired, funny, cheeky and flirty, but also poignant in places, expressing her longing for her far-away home. It was mesmerising to watch.

'You must be in the apparatus finals!' said Ellie and, sure enough, when Katya's score was posted she was in the top five on the floor.

'It is like a dream!' she squeaked. 'You must give me a big pinch to make sure I am not sleeping!'

'No sleeping now, Miss Popolova!' said Bella. 'We've still got the beam to go!'

As they faced the last rotation, it was clear that any chance of a team medal was long gone. But looking at the individual scores, Ellie realised with a shock that she and Memory stood a chance of making the all-around finals. Scarlett and Bella were lagging behind, and for the first time ever Ellie saw Scarlett looking completely panicked. She'd never displayed an ounce of nerves in competition before. She had always been cool and composed, like an ice queen, but now she looked flushed and jittery. Even her beautifully-plaited hair had come loose around her face, and she kept throwing anxious glances up into the crowd.

'My parents are going to be furious if I don't make the individual all-around finals,' she said with a little shiver.

It was such a strange, sad thing to say that Ellie felt almost sorry for Scarlett. Ellie knew her parents would have been proud of her even if she came last, but she'd caught a quick glimpse of Scarlett's parents earlier – her glamorous mother, a carbon copy of Scarlett herself, dressed in designer clothes from head to toe and her dad, with a mobile phone attached permanently to his ear – and knew they were completely different from Ellie's own chaotic family.

Scarlett's beam was lovely that day, not as showy as usual, but more moving somehow, and it earned her a score high enough for the apparatus finals.

251

But it wasn't enough to earn her a place in the all-arounds. Bella also fell short by a few places, and Katya toppled off the beam on a very simple move.

'It's sometimes the way – you stick the difficult stuff and wipe out on the easy-peasy moves!' Vivian consoled her.

Of course, Memory gave a flawless performance. 'She's like a machine,' said Bella, ungrudgingly. 'She never puts a foot wrong.'

'But she looks as if she hardly cares,' said Ellie, feeling curious. 'I really, really don't get her. She just made all-around finals in second place, just behind Esme Mattari, but she looks as though she just lost a winning lottery ticket.'

'I guess she's gutted about our team score,' said Bella.

The GB girls had come in a disappointing twelfth place, and it was hard not feel that things could have been different.

But Ellie had somehow pulled her own performance round after her disappointing start. She stuck her beam and caused the crowd to gasp with her daring double turn. And that had put her in eighth place overall. Eighth! Which meant she was going to all-around finals with Memory.

It had been a weird morning. Tragedy for Eva and disappointment for Scarlett and Bella, but a chance to shine for Katya. And although the team competition might be over, tomorrow Ellie was going to try for the biggest title of all – European Champion.

CHAPTER
Thirty-Two

'Poor Eva! Tonsillitis!'

The girls were sitting in their shared dorm back at the hotel, running over the events of the day. After a quick hello to their families, Vivian had herded them all back for supper and an early night. There was no sign of Scarlett, who'd gone off with her parents after the event, but Memory was curled up on her bed wearing her usual pair of headphones and a scowl.

'Yes, poor Eva – she worked so hard and then she get a sniffle and it is all over – poof!' said Katya with a giant sigh.

'Sometimes gymnastics feels like the cruellest sport in the world!' said Ellie. 'No second chances, no room for slip-ups, no room for error.'

Just then there was a knock on the door. 'Do you think that's Vivian come to tell us off for talking after lights-out?' said Bella, pulling a face. None of them were quite as scared of Vivian as they had been, but nobody wanted to risk making her mad either.

But when Ellie opened the door she saw Scarlett standing there, with a tear-stained face and swollen eyes.

'My parents aren't staying,' she sobbed.

'Why not?' asked Bella.

Scarlett's face was red and blotchy. 'Because I'm not in the all-around finals.'

'But – you're in the beam final,' said Ellie.

'It's not enough!' said Scarlett. '*I'm* not good enough for them to stay.'

Ellie thought of the times Scarlett had boasted about the new leotards her parents sent her, the expensive gifts – but if they only showed an interest

255

when she came home with a medal, none of that really mattered.

'Oh Scarlett, you poor thing!' she said, putting her arms round her. She felt Scarlett tense fleetingly but then let go as she sighed in defeat. Ellie gave her an extra squeeze.

'That's tough.'

Both girls looked up. Memory had tugged off her headphones and was looking at Scarlett.

'Yeah, well it's OK for you!' said Scarlett, flushing with indignation. 'You're going to finals. Your parents must be *so* proud.'

'My parents . . .' Memory hesitated. She looked as if she was going to put her headphones back on, retreat into herself again and hide behind her usual scowl. But then she seemed to make a decision. She took a deep breath and said, 'They're not here. My mum and dad . . .' She swallowed as if the words were hard to say. 'They died in a car crash – a couple of years ago.'

Scarlett's whole expression changed. Her mouth fell open and the sour look disappeared completely. 'But – who do you live with?'

'My grandparents,' said Memory. 'I went to live with them in America after the crash.'

All the girls were silent for a second, taking in this huge piece of news. Why hadn't they known?

'So that's why you moved?' asked Scarlett quietly.

Memory nodded. 'I didn't want to leave Scotland. I hated America,' she said. 'But now all I want is to go back.'

'Why?' asked Bella.

Memory's eyes filled with tears. 'My gran,' she managed to say. 'She's – she's really sick . . .'

Katya sat down beside her and put a small arm around Memory's big shoulders.

'Is it bad?' she asked gently.

'Bad,' said Memory, the word little more than a sob. 'I found out just before the first squad camp.'

'Which is why you weren't exactly in the mood to talk?' said Ellie.

'Sometimes it's all I can think about.' said Memory, the words coming out in a rush now. 'Gran's having a big operation tomorrow. What if something happens and I'm not there?'

All the girls were silent for a second. Then, to Ellie's surprise, Scarlett got up and went to sit on the other side of Memory. She didn't put an arm around her and she didn't say anything; she just took her hand and squeezed it. Memory gave her a grateful nod.

Ellie realised then how wrapped up she'd been in her own concerns, and how silly those concerns seemed now. What was an injury or messing up your medal chances compared to what Memory had gone through – was going through? Suddenly she felt ashamed of herself, ashamed for not noticing what was going on with Memory and for not seeing how lonely Scarlett really was beneath all her bravado.

'Well,' said Ellie. 'I can't make your gran better, and I can't drag Scarlett's parents to watch apparatus finals, but I can promise you both one thing.' She looked around at the others, all of whom were clustered round Memory, their eyes filled with the same concern as her own. '*We're* not going anywhere, are we?'

The others shook their heads.

'You can count on us!' declared Bella.

'Exactly. Teammates are more than friends,' said Ellie. 'We're family. Always there for each other – no matter what!'

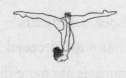

CHAPTER
Thirty-Three

'Memory told you, then,' said Lizzie the next morning.

'How do you know?' Ellie looked up in surprise.

'I was watching you all at breakfast,' she smiled. 'You looked like a proper team for the first time ever.'

Ellie smiled too. 'I'm glad she finally trusted us enough to tell us.'

'Memory's a lovely kid, you know,' said Lizzie. 'I remember before her parents died – she was as giddy as your pal Nancy.'

'Really?'

'Yup,' said Lizzie. 'But now her gran is really very

sick. It's touch and go whether she'll make it.'

Ellie sighed. 'We haven't been a great team so far, but we're all going to look after each other from now on,' she said. 'The whole squad is coming today to support me and Memory in the individuals.'

'Even Scarlett?' asked Lizzie, her eyes widening a little in surprise.

'Even Scarlett,' said Ellie. 'Oh, and I have an idea to help Memory. It was actually Vivian who made me think of it. I'll tell you about it on the way there. I'm going to need a marker pen, though – indelible ink. Do you have one?'

The atmosphere at the individual all-around finals was very different to the team event. There were only eight girls making their way around the apparatus today, so the arena was quieter and everything seemed more intense. Esme Mattari was the favourite, of course, but Memory was just behind her and the German twins, Gaia and Georgia, were in joint third, having achieved identical scores in qualification. Ellie had only just scraped her qualifying score, but because of her name the TV cameras seemed to follow her with as much interest as the top four.

'Don't mind them,' said Ellie to Memory, as the camera zoomed in on her whilst they warmed up. 'We stick together, OK?'

Memory nodded. She was very quiet again this morning, but less anxious somehow, as if telling her secret had taken a weight off her shoulders.

The rest of the squad were sitting with their families. Ellie could see Katya snuggled up next to Lucy, and Bella's mum chatting to her own dad. And there, in the middle of them all, was Scarlett. She was sitting between Mandy and Nancy and from what Ellie could see they were all laughing. Ellie had rung Nancy quickly that morning and explained that Scarlett needed to borrow her family for the day.

'After everything she's done, I don't see us becoming BFFs overnight!' Nancy had said sceptically.

'But now I get why she acts like she does,' said Ellie. 'And whatever's happened, she is our squad mate.'

'*Your* squad mate!' Nancy told her.

'Hey! You'll always be an Academy girl, Nancy Moffat,' said Ellie. 'And don't you forget it!'

'That's the biggest load of nonsense I've ever heard,' Nancy huffed, 'but I will babysit Scarlett for you. Only for you, mind!'

'Thank you,' said Ellie. 'Cos if rowing in the gig taught me anything, it's the importance of being a team!'

'What do I always tell you?' said Nancy. 'Boats know best. Now, what about Memory? How are you going to help take her mind off her gran today?'

'I'm not,' said Ellie.

'But I thought you said . . .'

Ellie had already filled Nancy in on all of the latest developments regarding Memory. All except one – her idea.

'She feels bad about not being there for her gran,' Ellie explained. 'So I'm going to help make sure that she is.'

'Um – how?' asked Nancy, sounding puzzled.

'OK, listen carefully,' said Ellie. 'Because I need you guys to help with this too.'

263

*

It was funny. When Ellie had dreamed of a moment like this, of being in the finals of a major world competition, she'd imagined sharing the stage with Nancy, Katya, Bella, or even Scarlett. But here she was, the only Academy girl to make it to the European finals, with a teammate she had barely spoken to until the day before. They were going round the rotations in pairs and so Ellie and Memory were in this together.

'Did you ever see any of the footage of Vivian competing at Euros?' she asked Memory as they warmed up together.

'Um – no,' said Memory. She kept glancing anxiously at her watch, and Ellie knew she was thinking of her gran, who was going in for her operation in just a few short hours.

'Well, she used to do this thing,' Ellie went on. 'She wrote messages on the palm of her hand – silly stuff like "Hi Dad!" or "That's how you do the vault!". Then when the TV cameras came around, she'd stick her hand right in their lenses so the world could read it.'

'Oh.' Memory seemed distracted, only half listening to what Ellie was saying.

'She did other crazy stuff too, like dancing and singing to the cameras, but I don't reckon I'm up for that, do you?'

Memory smiled for a fleeting second, and Ellie found herself thinking how pretty she looked when she was happy.

'But the hand messages were mainly for her family,' Ellie went on. 'So I had a thought. About your gran. Pass me your hand.'

Memory frowned. 'Why?'

'Because I know you wish you were there for her today,' said Ellie. She hoped that this was a good idea, that Memory wouldn't scowl and turn away. 'This way you can let her know that you are.'

Ellie reached out and took Memory's hand. Then slowly, very slowly, Memory unfurled her fingers and allowed Ellie to write.

CHAPTER
Thirty-Four

They were up on the bars first, always Ellie's strongest piece, and she'd never felt better. Knowing that she had the whole squad behind her, plus her family and especially Aunt Lizzie, made her feel invincible. As she landed she knew she'd made a fantastic start in the competition.

Memory also nailed her bars, and the TV camera man came in for a close-up as they stood waiting for their scores. Ellie slipped her arm around her teammate's shoulder and smiled. 'Ready?' she said.

Memory nodded.

'Together?' said Ellie.

'Together,' said Memory.

As the camera zoomed in, they both lifted their hands and opened their palms. There, written in black marker pen on Memory's hand, were the words, 'Love you, Gran.' And on Ellie's, 'Get well soon, Memory's gran!'

Ellie felt Memory's grip tighten on her shoulder. Glancing up at the big TV screen she saw their faces appear. Memory's eyes were filled with tears, although she was smiling bravely. The male presenter was saying something that they could just make out: 'Wow! What a great show of solidarity from the GB girls!'

'This reminds me of Vivian Ponting!' said his co-presenter.

'It looks like they're taking a leaf out of their coach's book here, sending a message to Memory Danster's grandmother. What a lovely gesture.'

'It must be tough on the young gymnast. She has the pressure of competing while she's also thinking of her gran,' said the female presenter. 'I'm sure everyone here in the arena joins her and the GB squad in sending their best wishes her gran's way.'

Just then the camera picked out the rest of the GB squad in the crowd. They had their arms around each other too, and as the camera focused in one by one they held up their hands, all covered in messages of love for Memory's gran.

Ellie thought she might cry herself, and she could feel that Memory was trembling, although her chin was up and she was still smiling bravely.

'Your gran will know you're there for her,' whispered Ellie. 'And that we are too!'

'All of us are!' said a voice from behind them. It was Vivian, busy drawing on her own hand. 'Nice trick, by the way – where'd you learn that, Little T?'

Then their scores came in. Memory had scored 14.6 and Ellie had nailed an incredible 15.1! Memory turned and hugged Ellie tightly. 'You were fantastic,' she said.

'And so were you,' said Ellie. 'Now, come on. Let's bring home a medal for the team.'

*

After that, the competition seemed to go like a dream. Both girls stuck their beam, and Ellie felt like her balance had never been better. Then her dynamic floor routine – which she performed with all her heart for Memory's gran – wowed the audience and earned her such a massive score that she suddenly found herself in second place in the leaderboard, with just one piece of apparatus to go.

'Ellie Trengilly seems to have found her form today after a mixed session yesterday,' the male commentator was saying. 'She really could be in with a chance here.'

'Yes, but vault was her weakest piece in qualifiers,' added his co-presenter. 'Will it be her downfall today?'

Esme Mattari was in first place, and Gaia Kopfler was just behind Ellie, with Memory trailing her by a tiny margin.

'You girls are both in with a serious chance here,' Vivian told them. 'You could both win a medal if you hold your nerve.'

But Ellie suddenly felt her confidence desert her.

Now that a medal was in sight, she felt sick, and the fact that she had to finish on the vault made it ten times worse.

'You need to go for the Amanar,' said Memory. 'A vault like that will bag you a score that Esme will never be able to match on the beam.'

Ellie shivered. She knew that Memory was right. If she could land the Amanar, she stood a chance of drawing level with the leader, or even topping her score.

'She's right,' Vivian agreed, 'Even a double Yurchenko won't do it. Mattari has a really high difficulty value on the beam. Even to be sure of staying in a medal spot you have to do your best vault ever.'

'I don't know if I can,' Ellie stammered.

'It *is* more of a risk,' said Vivian.

Ellie looked at her coach. She knew that they were both thinking of the day at the Olympics, more than ten years ago, when Lizzie had taken a risk and lost everything as a result.

'Sometimes you have to take a risk to win.' It

was Lizzie. Ellie hadn't realised that her aunt had managed to slip down to the arena – but now here she was. Ellie didn't think she'd ever been so happy to see her.

Lizzie glanced at Vivian. 'You do know that if I had my time again I'd do exactly the same thing?' she asked.

'Seriously?' said Vivian, her face crumpled with concern.

'Yes, so it's time you stopped blaming yourself for a decision *I* made,' said Lizzie. 'I was a big girl. Nobody forced me into anything – not even you.'

She turned and looked at Ellie. 'Gymnastics takes courage. Every time you let go, every time you fling yourself backwards, you are taking a leap of faith, trusting your body not to let you down, knowing that sometimes it will. Despite all the training, all the preparation, there are so many unknowns, so many factors you can't control. Look at Eva yesterday: a tickle in her throat and it's all over. Things can go wrong at any time, which is why you have to take the moments like this – when everything magically comes together – and give them all you've got.'

Ellie looked at Lizzie. She thought of all she had been through, all she had won and all she had lost, and she knew she was right.

'But the most important thing to remember,' said Lizzie, 'is that gymnastics isn't everything. If you've got friends and family who love you, then life goes on, even if you can't somersault ever again.'

Lizzie put her arm around Vivian as she said the word *friends*, but Vivian just shrugged it off and rolled her eyes.

'Did I ever say we were friends, Trengilly?'

Lizzie laughed. 'You know you love me really.'

'Ugh, forget this soppy stuff!' said Vivian. 'The great Lizzie Trengilly is right, as always – sometimes you have to take a gamble. Go all in – hold nothing back.'

'Then you'll have no regrets!' said Lizzie.

'But in the end it's your decision,' said Vivian. 'No one else can make it for you.'

Ellie glanced at both women. Sometimes she felt as if the ghost of Lizzie's past had haunted her whole gym career, but now she had the chance to lay that ghost to rest. This was her decision. Her career. Her ankle. Her moment.

As she took her place on the runway, she quickly glanced up in the crowd to where the GB group sat, waving their flags, their faces painted in red, white and blue. Nancy, Katya, Bella and Scarlett all had their arms wrapped around each other in solidarity – even Scarlett looked as if she actually wanted Ellie to nail this vault. Ellie's mum and dad sat beside them, with Mandy, and Bella's parents. Even the Senior Academy squad members were there, Sian Edwards and Sophia Mitford. And there was Tam, who'd first given her the courage to go for the Amanar, who'd coached her in the darkened gym and risked his own career to help her. He was winking at her, telling her to go for it.

They were all behind Ellie. This was her moment and she had to grab it with both hands – for Kashvi, for Eva, for Camille, for Nancy – for all the girls who *hadn't* made it this far, for every little girl who had ever dreamed of going to European Championships.

273

Ellie was the lucky one who got this chance. She had to do it for all of them.

And so, as the head judge raised her hand, Ellie took a deep breath and launched herself down the runway in what felt like slow motion. As she ran she recalled every single thing Vivian had ever taught her, every twist and modification of her body. She knew she was strong enough thanks to the gigging, and she knew she had the courage to go for it because she'd risked everything in the inlet to save those kayakers. And she knew if she failed then the world would keep turning.

She hit the vault and flew through the air, once, one and half, and into the second twist, round into the Amanar. Then she angled her body into the landing, pushed down with all she had. She seemed to hover in the air for a second and then her feet were down, her ankle juddered, she felt the pull of gravity and fought it with all her might as she lifted her hands to steady herself.

Afterwards, Nancy said that she looked like a giant wave suddenly halting at its midpoint, holding its white water miraculously steady just for a second. 'I've never seen you so strong!' she said.

And then it was over. Ellie raised her arm and stepped off the runway. Memory was hugging her and so was Lizzie. Even Vivian clapped her on the back.

They knew, before her score even came in – before Esme's was even registered – they all knew she'd done it.

And she had.

Memory's beautiful vault pulled her up into bronze medal position, just behind Esme Mattari. But in gold medal position – Junior European Champion – somehow, miraculously, against all the odds – was Ellie Trengilly.

CHAPTER
Thirty-Five

'What next?'

'The Olympics, I suppose.'

'I didn't mean that!' said Nancy. 'I was talking about what I wanted next at the all-you-can-eat buffet. That chocolate fountain looks awesome, but the cheesecake is also calling to me . . . decisions, decisions.'

Five days of competition were now over, and all the GB families were out for a big meal to celebrate. Sian had won the Senior European title, and Tam had a Junior gold that matched Ellie's hanging round his neck 'His and hers medals!' Nancy giggled when she saw them. 'Maybe you two are a perfect match after all!'

Katya had snuck in a bronze apparatus medal for her wonderful floor, whilst Scarlett had won the silver on beam. Memory had taken gold medal in vault, whilst Ellie had added bar gold to her all-around title.

'I refuse to even think about the next competition yet,' said Nancy. 'I swear my nerves can't take much more!'

'*Your* nerves,' exclaimed Ellie. 'What about those of us who are actually competing?'

'Oh, competing is easy,' said Nancy. 'Try being in the audience!'

Memory laughed. It made her look completely different, younger and less intimidating. She'd laughed a lot over the last few days. The 'Get Well, Memory's Gran' message had gone viral. Gym fans all over the world had posted their own messages of support online, written on their palms in dozens of different languages.

'She says she can feel all the love coming her

way,' Memory said. 'And the doctors say she's come through the operation far better than they expected. They don't believe it has anything to do with the positive energy but I do – and so does she!'

To top it all, the entire Popolova family had appeared on the day of apparatus finals, just in time to see Katya win her medal.

'They all ran here from circus when they hear I am competing!' Katya had said happily, as she introduced Ellie to her beloved brother Pietr, the world's smallest strongman, who promptly offered to lift Ellie up in the air with just his thumb.

'Um – maybe later!' she had giggled.

Scarlett's parents had sent her the biggest bunch of flowers ever, and a beautiful diamond pendant which she wore proudly round her neck, but Ellie couldn't help but notice the way she glanced at Katya surrounded by the bevvy of Popolovas (all of whom were as loud, crazy and energetic as Katya herself). Ellie knew she'd rather have her parents there than a thousand diamond necklaces.

'I do believe she's actually turning vaguely nice!'

Nancy observed. 'Miracles will never cease.'

'You might even miss her when she goes back to the Academy!' laughed Ellie.

'I'm going to miss you two more!' said Nancy, pulling a face. 'I mean, seriously, every time I start training up a new gig rower she gets nabbed for the Academy.'

The best news had been saved for last. Lucy had been offered a scholarship to the Academy. She would be starting in Beginner's squad at the beginning of next term.

Ellie didn't think she could possibly wish for anything more. Her little sister would be by her side at the Academy. Ellie herself was Junior European Champion, the highest accolade a Junior gymnast could achieve in her career. Next year she would become a Senior, so she could try to qualify for World Champs and even the Olympics.

And her aunt would be there for her too. Lizzie had announced that she was going to be both training and coaching at the Academy. 'So you'd better watch out, Little Trengillies,' she said to Ellie and Lucy. 'I can be ten times tougher than Oleg or Sasha – or even Vivian!'

'Three Trengillies in one gym!' said Vivian, rolling her eyes. 'What a nightmare!'

'No way!' said Ellie, her eyes shining with happiness. 'It's a dream come true!'

Acknowledgements

Huge thanks, as always, to the wonderful coaches, staff, gymnasts and families at Baskervilles' Gymnastics Club in Bath who continue to inspire, support, advise, help and generally put up with my nuttiness! Special thanks to the inspirational coaches Fran, Katy, Emma, Sasha, Levi, Rori, Maddie, Niamh, Vicky and Paul.

Thanks to David Merrick and all the members of the Helford River Gig Club for pilot gigging advice; to Neil Burton at British Gymnastics for endless patience with my gym questions; to Nick Ruddock and the GB Girls Junior National squad who let me come and watch them train at Lilleshall; to Simon Evans and all the BG merchandise stall gang for loveliness, coffee and cake; to Neil Fox from Milano for leotards, inspiration and book chats; to Louis Smith for letting me come to

training, and for reminding me of the key values
this sport can teach young people; to Kate Pocock
for sports injury advice, for being an inspirational
athlete and woman of wisdom when it comes to
elite sport (and much else, besides); to the fantastic
marketing and PR team at Egmont for everything
(with glitter on top); to wonderful editors Lindsey
Heaven and Ali Dougal for helping me make a
series I am proud of.

Most of all, thanks to all the girls and boys who
inspired this series and the friends and family who
always believe in me – especially Jonny, Joe (who
may only be a cameo but who fills a big place in
my heart) and Elsie, the small girl who once said,
'Tell me a story about gymnastics, Mummy!'
With all my love.